In Love with the Queen of South Carolina

A Country Girls Story by: Kasha Diaz

D1057217

Kasha Diaz

Prologue

KASHA

"I love you, nigga, but I cannot continue to put up with this shit! You think I'm dumb but you're playing yourself. I'm a made bitch understand this, Yayo! I never needed you nigga, I wanted you!" I screamed as I watched him with tears in my eyes pulling off in the brand-new Maybach, I bought him. *"I'm a Made Bitch! Remember that!"* I said more to myself than anyone, because this fool was gone...again!

Chapter 1

My name is Kasha Diaz and I'm a made bitch. Born and raised in South Carolina, I never really fit in. Not that I give a single fuck. But since middle school I stood out because I really didn't have homegirls, now homeboys I had by the boat load. By the time I made it to high school the girls hated me. It was only because I was cool with their man.

What the petty hoes didn't know was I'm the reason their niggas could buy them lunch and floss at the Jr high school football games. I was their plug, see it all started when my brother Duval got locked up.

He got caught with 100 pounds of loud and 300 bricks of the pure white girl on a private jet coming from Cali. The same trip he took twice a month for 2 years. They shipped his ass off with the quickness.

Gave my nigga football numbers on his first charge at 18. Straight bull shit. I remember that day like yesterday.

The bell rung as I was putting my blunt out in the female bathroom indicating six period was over and it was time to go home... "bout time" I thought. I made my way to the bus line high as a kite. I saw Mr. Taylor, my sixth period teacher, coming toward me so I ran towards the vending machine and turned my back. He walked past fast as hell and never saw me, so I got my money out because I had the munchies.

I got on the bus to take the thirty-minute ride to Santee from Holly Hill. Keesha's thot ass bumped into me on purpose and I dropped my salt and vinegar chips on the floor. "Bitch move", Keesha said as she continued to walk to her assigned seat like she didn't just bump me. I looked at the chips and felt the heat rise from my feet to my face. Before she got to her seat I was on her ass like a hog on slop!

Kasha Diaz

Now Keesha was at least 25 pounds heavier compared to my 115 pound slim frame. So, I knew I had to disarm this bitch, because if she grabbed me, it was over! With her back to me I grabbed her hoodie and pull it over her face. I gave her blow after blow before pinning her between the seats and going ham on that ass!

All I can remember after that was Ms. Jamison, the bus driver, pulling me off her and shutting the door to the bus in my face! I cursed her fat ass out and watched her scream in her phone for Principal Brown from the front office to send someone to help her.

By this time, I was kicking and punching the bus doors trying to fuck her up for touching me! "Fuck you bitch!" I screamed as I ran because I saw the DARE officer coming towards me. I hauled ass through the gates and straight to my Aunt Dot house.

In Love with the Queen of SC

I knocked on the door hard as hell, out of breath after running the half mile there.

"Who the fuck knocking on my got damn door?" My crazy ass aunt screamed.

"Auntie, open the door!" I screamed back.

"The hell your little po ass running from anyway!"

"This big girl tried me on the bus so I beat her ass." And Ms. Jamison grabbed me and threw me off the bus!" I said getting amped again.

"I know that bitch didn't touch you Kee?" Auntie said calling me by my child hood nickname. She was now putting on her Jordan 10s and pulling her long silky hair up in a bun.

See my Aunt Dot is a bad bitch. She had soft beautiful skin the color of mocha with long jet-black hair that she kept bone straight. Her body is on point with her flat stomach and big round booty and 36 double D perky breast. A lot of people say she remind them of Foxy Brown. She's an ask questions later type of gal! I've seen her beat three bitches up in the projects for fucking with her son, who is my first cousin Product.

I watched as my aunt grabbed her keys and cell phone prepared to beat Ms. Jamison down. "This your mama right here." she said as she looked at her cell phone walking down the steps. "Tonya I'm on my way to beat a bitch ass rat now for touching Kasha on that school bus!" She suddenly stopped in her tracks, whatever she said on the other end wasn't good.

I was confused as to why her hands started trembling and her soft grey eyes got watery. I've never seen her cry before, even when her husband Uncle Jr. was shot dead in their front yard, she displayed the human she is.

She never shed a tear in public and took over the family business with grace. See, Uncle Jr was that nigga in the South. He had every hood from South Carolina to Florida on lock with everything from weed, coke, pills, and heroin. He ran his business with an iron fist and didn't give a damn if you were two cents short, he would merk your ass!

One night his side chick Ms. Wanda came over to my aunt and uncle house raising hell! Auntie beat the bricks off her ass by the time Uncle Jr pulled up. Aunt Dot beat her so bad that Wanda ass was limping with her wig off to her car.

What they didn't know was the bitch went to her car and got her .38. She shot Uncle Jr 7 times before turning the gun on herself and blowing her brains out. When the cops arrived Aunt, Dot was kicking her corpse and screaming she was going to come to hell and beat her ass again.

"What's wrong?" I asked Auntie, pulling myself out of my thoughts. She was now leaning on her 2015 Audi.

"Duval is in a California jail." Her voice barely audible. I knew what auntie did for a living, I also knew my brother worked for her. I knew that

whatever happened wasn't good. Auntie kicked the custom Forgiato rim on her car.

"Well let's go get him, I know he's scared in there!" Auntie walked up to me and held me guiding my head to rest on her shoulder for a minute or two. She then grabbed my face with both her hands and pulled my face closer to here's, bending down and looking me in my eyes she said the realist shit I would never forget.

"You only fear God and nothing else. We are born to die Kee and in this life going to jail or dying is the price you pay to live debt free in this world! You can be a slave to the government now by slaving on somebody's jobs or take the chance on living life and being a slave in jail!" At 16 my life changed and nothing was ever the same after that! Shit just got real!

Chapter 2

"Where are you, Kasha?" I heard my home girl Ana scream into my iPhone.

I sucked my teeth. "I'm getting up now, boe."

"You should've been up its four in the afternoon if your ass wasn't trickin last night you would've been up," she said with a whole lot of attitude!

"The longer you sit on my phone the later I'm going to be, hoe," I said with just as much attitude.

"I'll see you in a minute." I hung up on her ass! She stayed talking shit but that's the only female I trusted with my life I thought as I peeled myself out of my king size bed.

I went into the bathroom connected to my bedroom and started to prepare for the day. I turned the shower on as hot as I could stand it and peeled my PINK panty, bra, and socks set off.

I lathered my body with my favorite coconut milk body wash and enjoyed the water on my soft skin. I finished up with my hygiene in the bathroom before I went to closet and decided to pull out a pair of light blue True Religion jeans and a white custom baby doll True Religion tank with gold rhinestones. I decide to wear my favorite Gucci gold sandals.

I applied my Mac Makeup on perfectly and added my custom chunky iced out Cuban link necklace, bracelet, and watch.

Pulling my 30-inch honey blonde and black Brazilian weave in a neat bun on my head, since I was headed to Ana to get my hair done anyway. I looked at myself in the full-length mirror and smirked. "Damn I'm sexy as fuck," I said out loud. I'm what some consider a dime and I knew it standing at 5'3 with a slim body, my ass was the biggest thing on me.

In Love with the Queen of SC

I have small, C cup perky breast. My grey slanted eyes are memorizing. People said I look like Keri_Hilson. I grabbed my keys "Ma, I'm out," I screamed headed towards the door. I hit the locks on my black on black Porsche Cheyenne truck, hopped in put my Gucci shades on. I turned the volume all the way up on Lil Boosie's Set it off.

YOU WANNA TALK SHIT? YOU WANNA RUN YOUR MOUTH?

YOU WANT SOME GANGSTERS FRONT YOUR MOTHERFUCKING HOUSE?

WE'LL SET THIS BITCH OFF, YEAH SET THIS BITCH OFF

WE'LL SET THIS BITCH OFF, SET THIS BITCH OFF

THEY CALL ME BAD AZZ, AND I'LL PUNISH YOU

YOU AIN'T MY EQUAL, WE AIN'T PEOPLE AND I AIN'T ONE OF YOU

SINCE '98 I GRABBED MY PLATE UP OFF THE LUNCH TABLE

I TOLD MAMA I'M THUGGING OUTSIDE WE DON'T NEED CABLE...

Kasha Diaz

I rapped along with Boosie bobbing my head headed on I-26 Charleston bound. Twenty minutes later I was pulling up to Ana's Salon. It was packed as usual and being that it was graduation weekend Ana had it jumping like a Gotti show!

I was proud of my girl doing her thing straight out of high school and already had her own shop! I fronted her the money 6 months ago when we decided to be partners and planned to open 20 salons across the south. Slayed was the first one we opened so far. We weren't doing too bad to be eighteen. Shit, Ana had already paid her half back. Straight hustlers! I walked through the door and looked around at the mayhem, it was at least 12 girls waiting.

"Well, well, well… it's about time you got here. Now I'm going to be running behind because you decided to be an hour late to your appointment," Ana said, rolling her eyes while motioning me to sit in her chair.

"Hey Ana, I missed you too," I said sitting in her chair as I noticed a chicken head looking at me crazy because I just walked in and was being serviced already, I guessed.

"Whatever, so you know we turning up tonight, right?"

"In real life, I'm too ready. I haven't been out in a minute," I said while checking my iMessage's. I noticed I had 5 missed calls from my boyfriend Shawn. I made a mental note to call him back after my hair was finished.

"Let his ass wait." I thought "I'll call his ass when I feel like it." I huffed under my breath.

Kasha Diaz

"Your mama still mad cause you didn't march at graduation last night?" Ana said, snapping me out of my thoughts.

"Hell, yeah she acts like I didn't graduate or something. I still got my diploma, so what's the big deal damn?" I said thinking about the big fight we had.

"Every mother wants to see her child walk down the aisle twice in life little girl," my mama said with a disappointing look. "It's bad enough your brother never will," she said.

"Ma, I told you I have to be in Miami. I'm still going to graduate; I'm just not walking. Bills have to be paid and walking in a blue ugly ass drape is not going to pay them," I said with a slight attitude.

I was now the breadwinner in my family. My mother couldn't work because she was still recovering from having a stroke and heart attack a year ago. That was the reason my brother Duval had to join the family business in the first place. He had to take care of me, our mom, and our younger sister Jewel and since we never met or saw our father, he had no choice. Since my brother got locked up, I started working for my Aunt Dot.

See it was either that or we all die because somebody had to pay the Mexicans back their money the Feds took off that airplane that landed my brother in jail. My brother never said two words from the time he was caught on the plane right up until them crackers told him he was going to serve a hundred years. He took it like a G. I cried for weeks after his conviction. My brother was my father and friend and I missed him terribly.

"All done," Ana said bringing me out of my trance. I looked in the mirror at my hair and smiled.

She had wand curled my entire head in twenty minutes and it was fire!

"Thanks boo, you know I love it, how much?" I asked digging for my wallet in my new Chanel purse.

"Chile please, buy me a drink tonight and bye," Ana laughed.

"You already know it's going to be bottle popping action all night," I slid a hundred-dollar bill in her apron.

"Call me when you're finish so I can come get dressed at your house tonight," I walked out the door.

My phone rang again for the seventh time since I got to Charleston. I fished around in my purse for it as I cranked my truck up. It was my dog ass nigga Shawn again!

"Yea, what's up?" I answered, sounding aggravated.

"I know you seen me blowing up your phone. Where the fuck you at?" Shawn yelled. I looked at the phone to make sure this was Shawn. Surely he bumped his damn head.

Who the hell he thinks he is talking to?

I hung slam up in the face and put his ass back on the block list. He got some damn nerves calling me questioning me like I'm his wife first of all and secondly, I knew the nigga was at his ex-Shanae house last night.

I had a sale in her apartment complex and saw the shit myself. I called his phone when I saw his Denali truck parked a couple units down from hers. He didn't answer but then I saw his dumb ass come out her door looking at his phone.

Looking sexy as fuck with his Robin Jeans outfit and Gucci shoes on. I watched as he went to his truck and called me. He didn't know I was there because I was in a rental car.

"Hey, you called me, baby girl?" he said sweetly when I picked up.

"Yeah, baby. I miss you. What you doing?" I said, playing along.

"Shit, over here at the trap, trying to get this change together." This man was lying through his damn teeth because I was looking directly at his ass.

Click!

I hung up on him.

He tried calling back five times before I watched him go back to Shanae's apartment and using a key to get in.

Shawn and I been going back and forth together for two years now. I met him right after Duval got locked up, at one of the high school games. He was eighteen years old, and had already graduated.

In Love with the Queen of SC

I was chilling with my homeboys, Joker and Diddy, in the parking lot on the hood of Joker's car at the game like always.

"I bet you twenty dollars Diddy, your ugly ass won't get Trina number tonight," I joked. I knew he had a major crush on her.

Diddy was black as tar with pretty straight teeth. He was six foot tall with muscles for days. He could dress his ass off. He was cute, he reminded me of Akon because he was black as hell just like him.

"Mannn, you been was supposed to put me in the mix," he passed me the blunt. I declined it because I just fixed my lip gloss and wasn't trying to get glitter on the blunt again like the last one.

"I don't do hoes, nigga. You know that if she ain't trying to cop a dime bag or something, she dead," I said as we all cracked up laughing.

"Joker, there go Shawn over there, go get him," Diddy said.

I looked over and, in my mind, I was like *dammn.*

Shawn was sexy as hell. His skin was the color of cinnamon. I watched as he walked over to me and Diddy like he was a boss nigga. He was rocking a pair of Robin Jeans with a white wife beater showing his entire tatted, upper body. His crispy white Air Forces set his outfit off. He had a Robin Jean hat on turned backwards. His thick eyebrows and strong jaw line complimented his baby face. When I noticed he had dimples I almost bust a nut right there. The diamonds in his watch and necklace were sparkling damn near blinding me. When he got closer, he dapped up Joker.

"What's happin', fool?" he asked, and that's when I saw his diamond filled mouth. My panties were soaked instantly!

"What's up, big family?" Joker asked. Shawn looked over at me and as I stood there eye fucking him, I smirked and nodded my head at him.

I was cute with my Jordan pink and white shirt I cut and tied it in the back so it looked like a baby tee. I paired it with my white Jordan tights and pink and white snakeskin Jordan 11s. My makeup and hair were on fleek like always. I was rocking it bone straight with a part in the middle.

"Damn lil slim, you like what you see," his deep baritone voice oozed with sexiness at me.

I shook my head yes with a sexy smirk on my face.

"Come holla at a nigga over here" he motioned toward his black on black BMW 745i.

I looked at Joker and he nod letting me know that Shawn was cool people. I grabbed my pink Jordan backpack off Joker hood and walked over to him.

"What's your name?" he asked as he walked me over to the passenger side of his tricked-out ride.

"Kasha, but everybody calls me Kash," I said as he opened the door for me to slide in.

He quickly made his way to his side and got in. He cranked up and I immediately reached for my pistol in my backpack and cocked it. I looked over at him.

His eyes got big as hell. "Lil slim, I'm just turning on the CD player chill," he said looking at me. "Oh, my bad," I laughed. "I have trust issues and don't fuck with too many people." I was still eye fucking him.

"I can understand that. How you know Joker and Diddy?" he asked while trying to find a station on Sir-us radio.

In Love with the Queen of SC

"I knew them all my life. We grew up together. After my brother got jammed two years ago, they have been holding me down ever since." I bobbed my head to the Migo's. He finally let the radio thump.

Trapped out the bando, got two like Rambo

Cop bird like birdman, got white like Lindsay Lohan

Made a hundred stacks off the pots and pans

On the corner serving grams, my niggas be on the block hard

My niggas be selling that hard, got bricks, like Shaq, at the free throw

You can call my phone, got them pricey for the LO, don't knock at my door, I don't wanna talk to you

"Who's your brother?" He lit up a blunt of OG Kush. I could tell by the smell that it was OG. I watched as he inhaled and wondered if that was the shit I had trafficked from Cali.

"Duval," I said taking the blunt.

He started choking hard. I mean like he damn near had me thinking he was going to die from coughing that hard.

"Yeah, this is most definitely my shit," I thought while hitting the blunt.

"You alright?" I asked with a half-smile.

"Duval is your brother? Wow, he was my connect. Shit ain't the same out here without him. How's he doing?" he asked, and I think he was trying to hold back a tear.

"He's cooling… he calls every day and I go every other weekend to visit him. He's in Texas now," I said as I thought about how much I missed him.

Shawn reached in his pocket and peeled two thousand dollars off a huge knot. "Put this on his books for me please," he gave me the money.

"I will," I looked at him as I smiled softly. I slowly grabbed the money and placed it into the smaller flap of my book bag.

We ended up talking and getting to know each other for an hour. I saw Joker walking over to the car so I rolled my window down. "You good lil sis? Are you still coming to the Waffle House with us, the game is over! He said laughing.

"Yeah, she good. We gonna meet y'all there," Shawn answered for me.

I nodded at Joker letting him know everything was good. I was all smiles. Shit, I would say the rest is history but it was the same typical shit a every hood nigga does. Wine and dine ya, fuck ya, and then start fucking up! The difference was I kept Shawn's ass around for a one reason. Nothing more nothing less.

Chapter 3

Club Vegas in Charleston on Saturdays was where the ballers went. It had three levels, so I rented out the top level for my family and friends to help celebrate me graduating. I pulled my truck up front and got out.

"Bitch, this isn't a parking spot," Ana said while cracking up laughing.

"It is, when you a boss," I flexed.

I tossed my keys to Tommy the security guard. Tommy also worked for me sometimes when I rolled through the hood on collection day.

"Hey, Tommy." I gave him a hug and he escorted us in.

Ana and I walked in the club and all eyes were on us. Ana was a pretty brown skin girl with perfect teeth. Her perky C cup breasts were sitting high in a custom Chanel gold bustier. Her round plumped ass was voluptuous in a pair of black Chanel high waist short shorts. She was rocking Gold spike gladiator Red Bottoms. Her hair was curled to perfection and I beat her face down.

I was rocking a red tailored jumpsuit that had a deep plunged neckline that had my breast sitting up high and hugged my ass. I decided to wear my diamond gold studded So Kate Louboutin heels. My hair was still wand curled and my makeup was perfect. I looked at my Cartier watch.

"Damn, it's eleven and this shit is bananas!" I yelled over the music to Ana.

"Girl, I'm definitely gonna find me a man tonight," Ana popped her ass to Nicki Minaj's *Feeling Myself.*

"Come on, let's check our section now so we can come back and mingle down here a little bit," I grabbed her hand and lead her towards the elevator.

When we stepped off the elevator, everyone raised their glasses.

"Aww, y'all so sweet," I cooed while walking around hugging everyone.

A pretty petite girl came over with sparklers on a bottle of Ace of Spade.

"Your table is over here, Miss. Diaz," she said as she smiled sweetly.

I handed her a hundred-dollar bill and she thanked me four times. I looked around for my Aunt Dot but didn't see her.

Since it was still kind of early, I didn't think anything of it. Ana was tapping her fingernails on the table indicating she was ready to go downstairs since our section consisted of my family young and older.

"Come on bitch, let's go," I shook my head at her.

"Hell yeah!" she said cracking up laughing.

"Y'all I'm going downstairs to party, order whatever, it's on me," I spat over my shoulder ready to get the party cracking.

"Well if I let you pay for everything, then what you need me for?" Shawn stepped from behind me. He took my hand and kissed it.

"That's where I gotta stop you, buddy... I don't need you!" I through on a fake smile. "Let my hand go and don't make a scene. I'll deal with you later, have a good night, Shawn," I walked towards the elevator.

"The food here is great," Ana said trying to play it off to my family.

We took off fast towards the elevator ready to shut shit down. The moment we got off the elevator, DJ Kub and DJ Major Boi dropped Rae Sremmurd and Nick Minaj *Throw Some Mo*.

Ass fat, yeah, I know.

You just got cash? Blow sum mo'

Blow sum mo', blow sum mo'

The more you spend it, the faster it go

Bad bitches, on the floor

It's rainin' hundred's, throw sum mo'

Throw sum mo', throw sum mo'

In Love with the Queen of SC

Throw sum mo', throw sum mo

I started popping my ass and grinding to the beat with Ana right beside me. We both started twerking down to the floor. All of sudden I saw hundreds, fifties, and twenty's come down around us. I looked back and it was this cute dude with dreads and a lot of gold jewelry on with piles of cash in his hand.

Aww shit, I thought as I twerked even harder.

Ana ass stopped dancing and was picking up the money. I was in my own world enjoying the music.

I hope buddy don't think we are pressed for no paper, I thought.

Personally, I don't do niggas that show off in the club. That shit brought too much unnecessary attention and trouble is always after that.

The waitress came over to me and handed me a bottle of Rosé'. I looked at her like she was crazy for a second. "He said enjoy", she said as she points to the dread head.

"Thanks, but tell him no thanks," I said as I handed it back to her and walked off.

"Who the fuck that nigga think we are? We shol ain't thirsty and we damn sure don't drink no cheap ass Rose," Ana expressed boldly, making me laugh hard as hell.

"Well why don't you let his thirsty ass tell you cause he's on his way with that bottle," I said looking in his direction.

"Excuse me, but you sent the bottle back, ma? I wasn't trying to holla, it's just I'm not from here and you two are the baddest I've seen since I've been here." He eyed both me and Ana. "My name is Yayo, I'm from Miami. What it do?"

Before I could respond, I saw Shawn out the corner of my eye headed over to us.

"Kasha, what the hell is up? You not about to be in no nigga face, disrespecting me!" He yelled so loud I saw people turn to look in our direction.

"Yo, homie chill. I was trying to buy them a bottle, but they sent it back and I came to ask why!" Dread Head said, holding out the bottle.

Shawn looked from him then to me.

"Get your dumb ass out my face nigga before shit get real," I said through clinched teeth.

Shawn grabbed my arm and was about to pull me, but Tommy walked over and gave him a dead stare. He knew what it was hitting for because he went and sat his dumb ass back at the bar.

"His ass is definitely cut the fuck off!" I said to Ana who was cracking up laughing.

"Yooooo, Tommy was about to Donkey Kong Shawn's ass." Ana was leaning over laughing. I was pissed so I excused myself to go to the ladies' room.

"I'm coming because I don't need Shawn kidnapping you," she teased. I rolled my eyes and headed to freshen up with Ana on my heels.

I checked my hair and makeup, and took a couple deep breathes to calm my nerves. I reached for my wallet and pulled out a pre rolled blunt. I lit it and let the drug soothe my nerves.

"Ok, let's turn up!" I switched my ass towards the bar.

We ended up popping ten bottles that night, drunk wasn't even the word for us. My bodyguard Tommy ended up driving us home. Around 3:45 in the morning I made it through the door and crashed on the couch. The entire room was spinning before everything went black.

Chapter 4

It was four thirty and my house phone rung almost simultaneously with banging at my door.

"Who the fuck is it?" I shouted, not caring who it was. I jumped up realizing I fell asleep on the couch.

"Open the door, Kasha, now!" Shawn yelled back.

I blew a loud breath and snatched the door opened.

"The fuck you want, nigga?" I gave him much attitude, folding my arms.

"What's wrong, baby girl? Why you switching up on me? You don't love your number one nomo?" he questioned, reaching for me. I slapped the nigga's hand away from me and took a few steps back.

"Nope I don't, it's over, bruh," I slammed the door. I snatched it back open fast. "And if you knock on this fucking door again, your mama gonna bury for ass." I slammed it back shut.

"Nigga waking me out of my sleep," I mumbled on the way to my room to get in my bed.

I took a quick shower not even bothering to put on clothes afterwards. I laid down and prepared to go back to sleep when I heard banging on the door again.

I threw the covers off me forcefully, grabbed my .44 for under my pillow, threw on my silk Fendi robe, and charged towards the door. Cocking my pistol, I snatched the door open, pointing my pistol directly at who I thought was Shawn.

"Ram, why the fuck is you here five in the morning?" I lowered my gun.

The look on his face was unreadable but something definitely was off. Ram was my right hand in the streets. He was known to knock a nigga out with his one hitter quitter. He stood 6'4 and was built like a linebacker. He had a cute baby face that he kept in a deadly snarl. His name rang bells in the streets since we were eight. That's when he caught his first body.

Kenny was a neighborhood stick up kid who decided he wanted Ram's bike. Long story short, Ram killed him by beating him viciously with a cinder block. Nobody snitched because they knew Ram's dad Pedro would merk anything moving the wrong way if they did.

"Put something on now, somebody just burned down the spot-on Hilliard!"

Power walking back to my bedroom, I slipped on my black Trap Gang hoodie, black matching sweatpants, and my black Timberland boots. I grabbed my desert eagle from on top my closet and darted towards Ram, locking the door behind me. Hilliard street was two streets over so we decided to walk over there. I saw the flames blazing walking from my back yard.

"Shit...fuck...! It's thirty pounds of loud in there, nigga. What the fuck happened?" I asked through gritted teeth, looking over at Ram.

"What the fuck you think, somebody burned it down. Shit I was at Renee house! Corey and Scooter said they ran to get something to eat from the Waffle House. When they came back the shit was on fire. They walked up to the porch and saw someone wrote die slow in red spray paint on it." Ram walked over to Corey and Scooter who was parked in a black Lincoln town car on the dirt road one street over from the spot.

I was pissed but I couldn't blame Corey and Scooter for what happened. They were loyal to me and shit I guess they are allowed to eat, *right?*

"Give it two weeks and then put a reward out if we haven't figured out by then who did this," I said leaning against the car smoking my Black and Mild.

"*Two weeks?* That's too long. The streets gonna think we soft as fuck if we wait that long," Scooter said rolling up a blunt of sticky.

"If we put one out now, do you know how many lies we're going to have to go through cause Ray Ray and Ty Ty daddy need pampers? Nigga, we play chess not checkers," I said looking him in the eye.

"Ooooh yea, that's smart," he said looking up like he was really thinking about it.

I shook my head as I continue to watch the police and firefighters try to secure the scene.

"Somebody's mama is gonna be eating collard greens and macaroni after she bury her child," I said out loud to no one in particular.

"Huh? What does that mean?" Corey asked, sounding confused.

"Somebody is going to pay with blood for this," I said smiled an evilly. Something I did when I was really pissed off.

"Ram, I didn't see Aunt Dot at Club Vegas tonight, where is she?"

"I've been calling her but she ain't answer," he said pulling his phone out to dial her again. "No answer," he said dialing her again.

"Well it's six in the morn, she's probably sleep now dickhead," I said standing up straight to leave. "Y'all go home and get some sleep and I'll hit y'all in a few to tell y'all where to set up later," I said leaving them to their thoughts.

"The hell Auntie at?" I asked myself as I reach my back door.

I'll find her when I get up, I thought pulling off my clothes preparing for bed.

****

I woke up four hours later feeling groggy. I reached over to find my phone when I realized I never got it out my purse last night. Peeling myself out of bed I dragged into the living room to retrieve it. I flopped down on the couch and got it. My eyes bucked out my head when I saw 36 missed calls.

Shawn ass is tripping, I thought.

As I scrolled, I realized most of the calls was from Auntie's phone. I hit her contact immediately, she picked up on the second ring dumbing! "Why can't you answer your phone! I've called the house and blew your cell up. Meet me at the number one spot asap!" She screamed then disconnected.

"Well good morning to your ass too, Auntie," I said to myself because the heffa hung up on me. "Another Day, Another Day," I sang on my way to the shower.

Chapter 5

We pulled up at the French Quarters Hotel downtown Charleston in two black on black Tahoe's a few hours after my phone call with Aunt Dot. Hopping out the truck with Tommy's assistance, I walked in the entrance like I owned it.

The concierge, Ethan greeted me by name, "Hello Kasha, it's always a pleasure," he stated as he kissed the top of my left hand.

"Like wise," I stated with a professional smile and slight bow.

"I'll show you the way," he said as he turned on his heels.

Stepping in the elevator I mentally prepared myself for whatever was coming my way. "Here we are Ms. Diaz", Ethan expressed in his deep French accent, standing in front of the elevator door.

"Merci," I smiled and winked because he taught me how to speak French over the years.

I walked to room 622 and pressed the bell and waited for Auntie to answer.

Aunt Dot owned half of the hotel; this was where she held all *family meetings*. Only the trusted knew about this room. From the outside it looked like a regular room, but the entire sixth floor was room 622. Listen, nothing but 22,000 square feet of exquisite furniture and drugs were inside. Along with heavy artillery *of course.*

There was a goon positioned at every entrance along the hallway inside and out. Shit was ten times more locked down than Fort Knox. Walking in after Auntie opened the door for Tommy, Ram, and I, she switched over to the wet bar.

"Patron or Screaming Eagle?" she asked while pouring herself a glass of the twelve thousand dollar bottle wine.

"Actually, have room service bring me a glass of Armand de Brignac with a splash of orange juice, a bagel with honey pecan spread, and fresh fruits please," I said with a smile plastered on my face.

After ordering my requested meal she ushered us to the office setup in the west wing of the room. "Kasha, your ass is getting on my nerves with not answering the damn phone!" Auntie said while rolling her eyes.

"Understandable, but we have a problem auntie! Last night the Hilliard spot was burnt down. We took a loss, a 300 pounds loss that is. This is some bull shit, then to make matters worse the goons said they saw "die slow" written on the porch" I stated catching her up on the latest events.

"Well, that's what this meeting is about." Auntie replied.

Taking a deep breath and looking me directly in my eyes she continued.

"We're at war with the Gwolas! It's no turning back, they have decided to up the price on everything and is now requesting twenty percent of all our profits, including the legal money. Of course, I declined, which prompted a call from Raúl. That fucker had the audacity to say, no isn't an option. I cursed his enchiladas eating ass out in Spanish." So, we have to now move accordingly." Auntie explained.

You see, Raúl was the head jefe of the Mexican cartel. Aunt Dot's deceased husband Uncle Jr had dealings with him for years. When he died Aunt Dot inherited the plug. Of course, he wasn't with a woman being head the family. That's the reason my brother Duval had to make the trips, which ultimately lead to him catching one hundred years. With Duval gone Auntie had to step in, and since then she's been fighting with the cartel for her respect.

I was now standing up from my seat pacing my Aunt's office.

"Are those fuckers crazy? Who in the entire hell is giving them twenty percent of our profit? They think we hustle for fun? Do they know who the fuck we are? They must've lost their fucking minds. I'm rounding all the goons up; shit we can go to war."

From the corner of my eye I saw Ram texting away on his phone with a deadly snarl. Knowing him he was putting the crew together to fuck some shit up.

"Raúl told me a member of our crew would die until the agreement is met. I don't take kindly to idle threats, so of course I took matters to another level," Aunt Dot said with pure evil etched on her face. I sat back down to hear what else she had to say.

Pushing a button that buzzed loudly Auntie said, "Bring it in…"

Wondering what the hell she had up her sleeve, we all waited in silence for a couple minutes. The door opened and in walks her right-hand man Bubba.

He greeted Ram, Tommy and I, then sat a large black steel box on her desk.

"Well!" Auntie stated with a smirk. "Here is taking matters to another level!"

I hopped up and unclasped the lock on the box, then slowly open it. Auntie then reached her hand inside and out comes a beaten fucking head of a Mexican woman. The bitch's eyes were still open, and her tongue was cut out. I backed up fast as fuck like the shit was a demon.

"What the fuck, Auntie?" I checked my clothes to make sure blood didn't get on me. Shit, I had on all white, *the hell was wrong with her*.

Ram and Bubba started laughing and poking at the head while auntie held it up by its hair twisting it around.

"This is Raúl wife's head, her body was nailed to the cross of their church's door. He wants to play God, then I'll show him I'm fucking Mother Mary!" she said without even smirking.

"Yea, we're definitely at war. Your ass been around those migo's too long, chopping off heads and shit," I laughed.

Auntie ass is crazy as fuck and they should've known she don't play about "The Family." The last time we had beef, Auntie had the goons dig up corpses of their deceased ancestors and mailed it to them. Needless to say, our old enemy heard her message loud and clear. That was after she had every boy killed in their family over the age of twenty-one. Her ass is pretty but she's loco for sure.

"Ok, so now that we're officially at war, we are moving everything around, effective today. Ram call every head person of each trap and shut it down. Everything is to be moved to their designated warehouse until further notice." Auntie gave out orders like that boss she is.

The intercom buzzed and the butler let us know my food and drink request was here.

"Can you at least move that bitch's head until I finish my food?" I rolled my eyes. Auntie had the head sitting on her desk like a damn picture frame.

"Yeah, I guess I can," her evil ass responded. Earl, the butler, rolled the trolley in with my food and I was ready to dig in.

The liquor from the night before still had my stomach doing flips.

"So, how are we supposed to make money, when every trap is shut down?" I asked taking a sip of my mimosa.

"Which brings me to the next subject, my niece darling," she said gazed at me.

Awww, shit, I know this about to be some dumb shit, I thought to myself.

"Just know I don't sell ass," I said, and everybody cracked up laughing.

"I have someone you need to meet," she said while standing up and disappearing through the door.

A couple minutes later she returned with someone in tow behind her. Looking up from my brunch, my eyes went to the dude with Auntie. My gut instincts immediately told me he wasn't to be trusted. I discreetly rubbed my hand over my back where my Beretta U22 Neos .22 LR Semiautomatic rested.

This is always my weapon of choice when I'm handling business, because I could hide it easily. The stranger and I made eye contact; he was the first to break it. So, I knew for sure this dude was a snake.

I made a mental note and turned my attention to my aunt for an explanation. "This is Yayo from Miami our new connect, Yayo this my niece and top enforcer Kasha," Auntie said taking her seat behind her desk again.

Yayo? Yayo? Where do I know this nigga from? I thought to myself.

He reached his hand out to shake mine, but I motioned toward my food. Making him think I didn't want to shake his hand because I was eating, when in reality I just didn't want to.

"My bad shawty, it's nice to meet you," he had a mouth of gold.

My only response to him was, *"Likewise."*

"Kasha, you're going to go with Yayo and setup shop in Miami. I think it's best we find new territory. With the help of Yayo we can take that city over too. That way we can handle the war here, and still get money," Auntie stated while popping a bottle of Ace of Spades.

She poured each of us a glass then raised hers.

"To new beginnings," we all chanted after Auntie.

Looking at Yayo from the corner of my eyes, I promised myself I was going see what is up with Mr. Yayo. You can bet your last dollar on that shit!

Chapter 6

After speaking with Auntie, I decided to have a meeting with the squad. I needed everyone to have their eyes opened. Hell, Auntie killed the head Jefe's wife so I knew shit was about to get real. Those crazy fuckers had us on their hit list for sure. I just hope they didn't underestimate us, that would be a deadly mistake.

Over the years we have accumulated strong alliances. Including the Jamaican Posse, the Latin Kings, and the Black Guerrilla Family, just to name a few. It was nothing for us to go to war, so I couldn't understand why Raúl wanted to fuck with us. "His ass will learn today!" I thought. I pulled my truck up to One Love, a Jamaican restaurant in the hood and parked.

Walking in I was greeted by Dominic the owner. "Whaa gwaan nuh si yuh sence di daydah day," Dom spoke in his heavy Jamaican accent.

"Weh yuh ah she," I spoke back, *meaning how are you doing*?

We made a little small talk before I headed for the office here to conduct my meeting. Dom let us use a private room in the basement and in return we gave him protection. Not that he really needed it being as though his brother is a high ranked officer in the Jamaican Posse. Dom is also a close friend to Uncle Jr and Auntie. I believe he allowed it out of respect for my family.

Taking the flight of stairs down, I was greeted by all two hundred plus "family members." Them standing from their seat is a sign of respect and is required. It's been that way since Uncle Jr was in charge.

"You can have a seat," I spoke clearly. After they all took their seats, I began.

"It's been brought to my attention that the Gwolas and The Family is at war. Now I know you all have a lot of questions, but I'm going to give you instructions first, then I'll address your concerns."

I looked around the room making eye contact with everyone within my eyesight.

"Starting now, all traps are closed until further notice. We can't run the risk of losing more work during this war. So, think of it as a mini vacation. I also suggest that you and your family members be monitored 24/7. We gotta think like how we move when someone is on our shit list. Anybody can get it, and I refuse to bury any of you or your people." I paused for emphasis.

"I've brought in some enforcement from upstate to ensure you are all safe. You will still be paid your weekly salary. If you can get out of town until you are contacted, please do so. If not, stay after the meeting to be assigned to a safe house for you and your family. Tommy has a new cell phone for each of you, they will be given out upon your exit. DO

NOT contact anyone from that cell except your lieutenant. The Gwolas are notorious for tracking cell phones during a war. That's always been their M O. They also know we are heavy and unstoppable damn near. They will come in packs, so do not underestimate them. Now, any questions?"

Almost immediately Lil Peanut who ran the Pineland area stood up.

"Why are we at war with the plug? I mean I trust that you will make sho we eatin, but damn. That's some crazy shit, fo sho!" he expressed, and then took his seat.

"I know this is the same question you all have. I'm gonna keep it one hundred with y'all. It all boils down to them not liking a woman in charge. Raúl told Auntie they were upping the price and they wanted twenty percent of our profit. As if he wasn't already tripping, he also said a family member will die until we agreed. So, we gotta make sure you guys are safe."

The room erupted with chattering; The Family was in cahoots with our decision to choose war. "Man, fuck Raúl!" I heard a couple people say, I knew they all would be ready for whatever. "Any more questions?" I asked before glancing at my watch.

Fresh from the Vill, stood up and the room went quiet again as he spoke. "So, do we have another plug, being that this one is gonna get smoked?"

The entire room shook with laughter.

"His ass is definitely getting smoked, but yes we have one already. You know we play chess, not checkers, nigga," I said with a smirk.

After answering a couple more questions, I excused myself from the meeting.

Ram and Tommy finished up for me. Walking to the front of the restaurant I saw Dom had my plate ready.

"You know me oh so well, my friend." I took my plate and gave him a peck on the cheek.

In Love with the Queen of SC

Opening the to go tray, my mouth watered looking at the ox tails, white rice, sweet cabbage, mac n cheese, and lemon cake. I was so hungry I opted to stay to eat it now.

"Hey Dom, I think I'm gonna stay and eat this, would you care to be my date?" I cheesed at him. Dom was in his early fifties, but didn't look a day over thirty-five years old. His salt and pepper dreads are always neatly pulled back in a hair tie. I could tell he was the man back in his day. His ice blue eyes probably got him all kind of pussy back then.

We took a seat in the back booth my uncle sat at when he used to come here.

"Dom, I might need your help with something. The Family needs another source to continue, *if you know what I mean...* Things are complicated right now, and you know I would never ask if..."

Don cut me off by placing his hand on mine.

"Shhhh," was his reply.

He stood up and went to retrieve a small black book from the floorboard behind the booth where we were sitting. Placing the worn book in front of me, in a hush tone he then said, "Dis belongs to yuh, it was left by Jr."

My interest was peaked.

"Thanks Dom," I said while putting the book in my Louis Vuitton backpack.

I devoured my food in record time and stood to leave. After saying my goodbyes to Dom and his staff, I headed home. During the drive from the restaurant to my house, I thought long and hard about my next move. Auntie's new connect didn't sit right with me. Just as the thought passed through my head, a lightbulb went off.

"He's the dread head from the club. That's where I know him from!" I said out loud.

My next thought was, what real plug goes to another state and makes himself known by throwing money. I was always taught the loudest person in the room, is the broke one! I was going to figure what it was really hitting for with him.

Pulling into my driveway, my phone rang and displayed private number. Rolling my eyes because I knew it was Shawn's ass. I decided to answer, and opted to take the call sitting in my truck.

"What, Shawn?" I answered him, clearly irked.

"Damn, I have to call my gal phone private for her to answer. That's fucked up Kash, why you doing a nigga like this?"

I sighed loudly because he sounded like a straight up bitch.

"Look, Shawn... I fuck with you, but you're a fucking liar. I watched you leave Shantee house the other night. I don't have time to go back and forth about it either. I'm not about to let you disrespect me with these bum bitches in these streets," I paused to catch my breath. "My nigga, should never give any bitch a reason to feel she has the upper hand on me. Especially when I gave you that same respect. So, from here on out, I'm just your boss. Let's just stick to the business, obviously you need to fuck off.

You're just not gonna do it on my watch." I broke it down as best I could.

"Damn, I guess I gotta respect that. I don't know why I do the shit I do, Kash. You're a good girl. I'm so fucked up in the head, I let these hood rats fuck up the best thing I had. Baby, please just forgive me this one last time. I wanna marry you baby. I love you for real, Kash."

I was rolling my eyes as I continued to listen. "You're my world, you're everything a nigga need." He said so sincerely. But unfortunately for him, I was all out of fucks to give.

"Nah, I'm good on that, I'll hit you tomorrow with your assignment ummk! Bye."

"I love y...." he started but I hung up and powered my phone off.

"Fuck off my line, bruh," I thought as I hopped out of my truck and headed towards the house.

Tat tat tat tat tat!

The sound of gun shots rang out. I immediately dropped to the ground as I felt the bullet penetrate my skin near my stomach, but I wasn't exactly sure where I was hit. My body went into shock immediately and my adrenaline was pumping, so it wasn't any pain felt at that moment that alerted me that I was shot. It was the metal slicing through my skin that let me know, it literally felt like the bullet danced around in my lower area. Going into survival mode, I grabbed my .45 out of my backpack and cocked it. Not knowing where the shots were coming from, I stayed low and focus to see where to aim. Spotting a dark colored car parked on the opposite side of the road fifteen feet away, I took cover and crawled in front of my truck.

Feeling lightheaded, I squeezed the trigger hitting the car with expert aim. Sparks flew every time I penetrated the vehicle, but I was losing blood by the second. Ram came from behind the house letting loose what sounded like a cannon. The sound of the vehicle's tires spun off loudly against the pavement and started to sound far away.

"You hit, Kash?" Ram asked. I could tell he was torn between seeing about me and going behind the car. The look in his eyes told me so.

"Yeah, my stomach!" was all I could get out before everything went dark.

****

Waking up to the sounds of Wendy Williams on a small TV in front of me, had me confused. Only for a moment, I had forgotten about last night's show down. Holy shit, someone tried to take your girl out. Looking around the room I realized, I was in the east wing of Auntie's hotel. The room was built for times like these. Auntie had on call doctors and a fleet of nurses in case any solider of ours needed medical attention. Bullets brought the feds, so we made sure to cover all angles and protect The Family.

"You're up I see!" Auntie came over with a plastic cup and straw that contained water for me and said. Pressing the button to slide my bed in an upright position, she fed me the water. It felt good against the dryness of my tongue and throat. I didn't stop drinking until the water was gone.

"How long have I been out?" I asked with a raspy voice. I sounded like a seventy-five-year-old smoking man with throat cancer. I tried clearing my throat a couple times before speaking again.

"Three days, almost four, being that it's almost midnight again." Auntie said taking a seat next to me.

"Damn, so give me the run down, y'all found the fuckers that shot me?" I started checking to see where I was hit.

Wiggling my toes, I silently thanked God I wasn't paralyzed.

"You're fine. The bullet did hit your spleen, which we removed. You'll be back up and running in no time." She filled me in on about my wounds, sluggishly. I could tell she'd been up worried because she always looked youthful, but not tonight.

"So, I guess The Gwolas thought it was that easy to get me, huh?" I snarled.

Auntie laughed at my gangster then continued to fill me in.

Apparently, Ram went loco while I was out. He called his brother Skrill, who is a fucking nut basket and was out for some serious revenge. The duo flew to Mexico, and blew up the village Raúl grew up in. Auntie said over six hundred people lost their lives. All because I was hit once. Now that's some fucking G shit right there. Only now I was more worried about Ram's brother, Skrill. It wasn't an off switch with him once he was started. He didn't care about shit, besides getting his whoever was on his shit list. He just wanted his target, unfortunately for Raúl, Skrill was out for blood.

My chest filled with pride as I thought about how hard my team went for me, but they would feel me personally. I couldn't afford to be viewed as weak, that would make me the target. I laid back and spoke with Auntie about that night, the parts I could remember. She had her own version that made me laugh because she viewed the security footage, and she said I was in G mode. Little did she know, Rual had awoken a beast he couldn't even imagine. The medicine I was given an hour after I woke up had my dosing off but my thought as I was doing so, PURE EVIL!

Chapter 7

For the next two days I chilled in the east wing of Auntie's room. Soldier after soldier came to visit me, with all kind of gifts. Each one told me they were ready to kick this war off. Still feeling a little sore, I was more than ready to get back to the money.

I was due in Miami four days ago and was beyond pissed. Auntie, being the boss pushed everything back until I was able to walk. The bullet tore my insides up and had me walking humped over. I'm too cute to be pushing a fucking walker to a meeting, so I'm going to chill. I cursed everyday about it and wanted to personally kill the fucker that shot me.

Ram was on it and told me when he came back, he would have the culprit brought to me. True to his word, I received a call around seven in the evening asking me to come to the Orangeburg warehouse.

Knowing exactly why, I hopped up and had my nurse help me dress in all black. The hour-long drive had me anxious, and my trigger finger itching. Pulling up to the abandoned building I was escorted inside. I was led to the back of the building by Tommy and Lil Peanut.

Stepping inside a small room I saw Ram and Skrill taking turns punching a figure. It was tied to a chair and gagged. As I got closer, I looked at the piece of shit and was pissed. This taco eating piece of shit was a teen girl. She had to be no more than fifteen years old.

"This is the bitch that shot me?" I asked to no one in particular. A sinister laugh escaped my throat. "You gotta be fucking kidding me! This tiny, punk bitch got the drop on me?"

I was now screaming. I had to give it to lil momma, she was gangsta for real. Being that young you would expect her to cry or plead. The bitch looked us all in the eye, as to say hurry the fuck up. Not shedding a fucking tear and not up for the dramatics you see in the movies with the talking and asking questions. I raised my .45 Beretta 4x4 Storm and squeezed the trigger until it was empty.

"Find her mother and father, I want them dead too," I said as I left out of the room.

I was exhausted when I arrived back in Charleston. My mind was moving a mile a minute, I needed a fat ass blunt ASAP. We definitely had to put a lid on Raúl immediately, this fucker really sent for The Family. I'm glad it was me that was shot, I didn't want any of my soldiers killed. They all wished it were them, anyone of them would've taken the bullet in a heartbeat.

We really are a family, so I made it my business that everybody ate. Everyone looked out for one another. I needed to get to Miami to seal this deal with the new connect thought, so I can make sure my family continued to eat. Fuck sitting around waiting to heal, I was leaving tonight!

"Auntie, can you have Tommy swing by to grab my clothes? I'm leaving for Miami tonight." I limped to the closest chair to rest my aching body.

"Are you sure? I mean, you don't want them to see your injury as you being weak. We already get that because we're women," she schooled me.

"Exactly why I'm taking my ass tonight, we are just as much of a boss as them. I'm going to this meeting with a bullet in my stomach. How much more gangsta can I be?" I looked her in the eyes. Knowing when not to challenge me she started calling out shots to prepared with leaving.

"Very well, it's settled. I called to get everything gathered. Go rest while I finish getting things in order," she said leaving me to my thoughts.

Stepping back in the room shortly, she made me the happiest gal in the world when she told me Product was here. Product was Auntie's only child; he was ruthless as they come. Auntie defaced him at the age of ten. Meaning he never had his picture taken. Never had his fingerprints taken, he's basically nonexistent on earth. He was home schooled and started training to be a savage at six years old. She had him running things out in Memphis. Nothing moved in any way without his consent.

After laying his murder game down, everyone realized he meant business. Little cousin had more bodies then a cemetery for real. So, him coming to Carolina wasn't to just check on his favorite big cousin. I knew he was gonna tear some shit up, and even I was nervous! Stepping in carrying pink orchards and a small yellow teddy bear. I stood to my feet, ignoring the pain in my abdomen.

"Product!" I shouted. The smile etched on his face confirmed he missed me just as much.

I grabbed him in a tight hug with tears streaming down my face. That's how much I loved and missed my cousin. We haven't seen each other in over 4 years. Shit, with the mass destruction he left here around that time, it was best he didn't contact us often.

"Damn, baby girl. I missed you," he said, then his eyes changed to a darker black as he continued.

"The people that hurt you, I'm going kill them, Kee! I'm gonna murder their entire blood line, I promise." He expressed, calling me by the nickname he gave me.

"I know P, but I'm good. Just don't do anything reckless, ok? Promise? I took care of it, I swear. I need you to keep a low profile while you're here. How long to you plan to stay?" I asked still holding on to him. I missed the nigga that taught me to keep my head held high no matter what. I was a thorough bred because of him and Auntie. They hardened my heart, and perfected my hustle, I'll forever be indebted to them.

"Until you don't need me Kee, I'm not leaving this time. If I'm gone it's because y'all gonna have to bury me. I've been away too long, and these mother fuckers need to know, y'all are untouchable! You understand?" he looked me in the eyes.

I shook my head yes, and placed my head back on his shoulder, still holding on to him. When Duval left, Product protected me. He made sure I knew my worth and what I was put on this earth to do. Now that he was back, I planned to implement him in my world to the fullest. I would just have to keep a close eye on him, because things tend to get bloody when he's involved. Product, Auntie, and I went down memory lane for hours about how far The Family had come. Even though Product wasn't with us in the flesh he always was in the loop about everything.

Shawn calling my phone prompted me to fill my team that he was no longer apart of the street team. I opted not to take his call, but I did assign a member to pay him a visit soon. I didn't want any beef with him, but I had to leave him in the past. Shawn is dead weight at this point, and after this shooting incident, I refuse to waste any more precious time.

Chapter 8

The flight to Miami gave Product and I much needed bonding time. I learned that he was expecting a baby boy soon, and he wanted to marry his mother, Jules. That was surprising since P wasn't the most trusting person when it came to females. I was more than ready to meet my soon to be cousin though. I've convinced him to have her fly to Charleston the moment we got back. I took a bet, a threat, and a joke to get him to agree, this nigga was still difficult.

"So, this Yayo character rubs me the wrong way. I gave him the family stare down, and he failed," I put Product up on game.

"He only has one time to show anymore red flags, and he's dead," Product stated nonchalantly as the plane descended.

Twenty minutes later we were being ushered into a black Phantom. Yayo dapped Product up, then extended his hand to me. Not seeing a way out of the bullshit handshake, we shook hands. As soon as our fingers touched, a jolt of electricity shocked us both. With us both obviously stunted, I snatched my hand back quickly.

"I heard about your recent incident shawty, you straight?" Yayo asked, but this time looking me directly in my eyes. I could tell he was wondering what the hell just happened with our hands. Making sure I never broke eye contact with him, I stated.

"I'm tougher than I look, shit happens but it will never happen again."

Again, he looked away first.

Weak ass nigga, I thought to myself. My mind drifted back to our half handshake.

The seats were leather, so it wasn't a static pop, although it felt that way. I turned my attention to Product who was looking at Yayo suspiciously. I'm pretty sure he peeped his broken eye contact with me.

Since we were preteens Uncle Jr taught us a man that can't maintain eye contact with us, wasn't to be trusted. His father had taught him that, so he passed it on to us. He taught us to still do business but never give them a chance to cross us. Just ensure we check their background thoroughly. His teaching kept me protected and rich so far, so I'm definitely still following it.

After digging into Yayo's life, which I had Ram do the moment he left Auntie's office. I found out he is very powerful man in Miami. He's of Haitian descent, twenty-nine of age and very dangerous. I could only find information of him as an adult, starting from age eighteen.

It was as if he just magically appeared at that age. No birth certificate, social security number, school records or driving license. According to my research he still doesn't have any of those things. His real name was Anel Saintilmon, and he'd been in Miami for six years now.

"So, Anel what is it about you that I need to know?" I asked, revealing that I knew his real name. Chuckling before responding, he made sure to look me square in the eye.

"Seems to me you know more than I care to tell, so I'll let you figure it out," he said staring intensely.

Not sure what to make of his response I turned my attention to the window. We were pulling up to a gorgeous mansion. It looked like something off a cartel movie, with all the giant palm trees humorous lawn, and most importantly armed guards.

It's all tucked behind a tall iron gate, with more armed guards at each post. I noticed snipers on the roof, so I made sure my trusted dessert eagle was close by. Shit, not that I'll stand a chance against this shit but hey, I would pick off at least one of them fuckers if I was going go out.

I guess Product picked up on my uneasiness because he grabbed my arm.

"You good, cousin?" he asked with his eyes trained on Yayo. Not bothering to respond I watched as Yayo downed the window for the guard that approached the car.

"Everything is everything," he said to the worker.

The gates opened.

After what seemed like forever, we made it to the top of the driveway. No one spoke a word as we exited the vehicle and made our way into the gorgeous home.

Upon entry, we were greeted by his maid.

"Whatever you need I'll be at your every beck and call," she stated with a smile that made me feel at ease. Regardless of how much this bitch cheesed, I was still gonna be on point.

The house was anything short of royalty. My jaw dropped as I stepped further into the home. The floors were white with gold flakes the size of goldfish. *Wait, it was goldfish swimming in the floor…*

The artwork that adored the walls look like they belonged in a museum. They mostly were black men and woman, some wearing crowns, some looked Godly like. The maid gave us a tour that lasted forty-five minutes.

Every room was decorated in the finest. In total, Yayo's home had seventeen rooms, with seventeen bathrooms. He had a theater room, inside basketball court, and a guest house by the pool. His kitchen was fully equipped with three chef's and he had 6 maids on duty at all times. Yeah, he was really doing it big and now I wanted into this business Aunt Dot said he owned. Shit, I wanted to live like this, and I'm considered rich! Yayo told Product and I that we could choose any room on the second floor, so I decided on the all black room. It had a California King bed with a huge glass chandler that hung above the bed. The black decor made it sparkle and lit it the room beautifully. The meeting was still scheduled for this evening, so I prepared to get ready for it. Hopefully, everything goes smooth, and I'm on the next thing smoking back to South Carolina.

Chapter 9

YAYO

I watched as Kasha made herself at home in my seventeen-million-dollar home. Let me introduce myself. The streets know me as Yayo, and for good reason I am the king of cocaine.

I was born and raised on an island called Hispaniola in Hatti. I know you probably never heard of it. It's near the Dominican Republic and is the holy Mecca for drug smuggling.

At the age of six I was taught the drug smuggling business from my pops. See, pops was the head of the Haitian Military, and a ruthless mother fucker. I've witnessed him kill people for just about anything. He taught me to get rid of anything that would pose a threat in anyway. Like a sponge I absorbed everything and grew to be just as ruthless as my pops. At the age of eighteen I moved to the states, Miami to be exact.

Well, since I'm telling my story I'll tell you the truth. I decided I wanted to see where all the drugs go after we package and ship them. Pops always told me that people get rich off of the cocaine in the states, but as far as I could tell we wasn't. I won't say I was living like the kids you see on TV, but we definitely weren't rich. I couldn't understand how we could make others rich off shit we sent to them. So, shit I was going to where people were getting rich, fuck it. I remember the day I left like it was yesterday.

"Come boy, it's time to go!" my pops yelled at me through my small bedroom window from outside. It was four in the morning, but I had already been awake for two hours. I grabbed my backpack I packed and prepared to leave. I went to my mom's room as I always did each morning.

"Mom," I said just above a whisper.

"Anel, my sweet boy, come."

My mom reached over to me from her bed. She knew this would probably be the last time she saw me for a while because she helped me plan to leave.

"Remember family is first, ok. I want you to go to America and be better than your father." She continued as she stroked my face and then placed kisses all over my hand.

"I will momma, I'll be back for you soon, promise, ok?" Giving me a toothless smile, she stared at me intently.

"Ok baby I know." I kissed her face and hurriedly left her room to join my pops in his Prang truck.

"What took you so long?" he asked as I placed my backpack on the floor.

"Ma wanted me to get some supplies before we come home tonight." I lied with a straight face. He replied with a hard "Hmm."

The twenty-minute ride to our warehouse was silent as any other day. My pop wasn't the type of man to talk just to talk, but when he did spoke it was all knowledge. I just couldn't figure out if he knew so much, why he had so little.

Pulling into the warehouse garage we both exited the truck and walked into the 100,000 square foot building. More than one billion metric tons of pure heroin and cocaine was stored and distributed there. 17,000 troops worked busily around the clock while being paid 5.00 an hour. Now that I think about what the fuck, yo, our own people were shitting our asses. But anyways, back to my escape.

I reported to my assigned station and dapped up my right-hand man Punch. "Man listen I'm ready to get the fuck out of here for real!" Punch said as he looked around to make sure no one heard him.

"Is everything in place? There's no turning back now," I whispered back to him.

"Yea, I did everything you said and I also grabbed two AR's from my pops." Punch let me know.

Punch was hungry like me, he and I planned this day since we were sixteen. We agreed that his strong suit was numbers, the nigga is smart as fuck. Me, well I'm the enforcement, I'll lay anybody the fuck down.

We both worked silently until we heard the horn that signaled our first break. Grabbing my backpack punch and I headed to the ground level of the warehouse and prepared to start our mission. Pulling two life-size bags from my backpack, the same we use to smuggle the drugs on the boat. Making sure the oxygen masks we working I gave one to punch.

"Don't turn it on until we are inside the crate, get dressed," I instructed as we both dressed in police uniforms and tossed our other clothes in a nearby dumpster.

We both snuck onto a freighter and hid, turning the life-size bag inside out, we zipped ourselves up along with the oxygen mask. Phase one was completed now we had to make it through customs. The freighter we were on had a million dollars' worth of coke on it. The coke was stored inside with looked like mango, so we knew customs wouldn't be a problem.

Two hours later the boat came to a stop and we both sprang into action. Zipping ourselves out of the bag, we grab the AR's Punch stole from his pops. Two armed guards were walking in our direction, so we both prepared to be checking the product as if we were with customs. Then when customs came, he pretended to allow them to check the packages. After the officer said everything was good, I signed the forms as if I had authorization.

"That was close, brudda. I thought they was going to kill us," Punch said as we zipped ourselves back into the bags. Putting the mask on, I set the timer on my watch for three hours, then he would move on to phase two.

After what seemed like a short time later, my watch indicated it was time to move, we would be in Miami in a few hours so I had to move quickly. Unzipping the bag again, I let Punch know it was time.

"Punch, I know you hear me, hurry the fuck up and get up NOW!" I said angrily.

This nigga sleeps harder that a baby! I thought as I unzipped Punch's bag.

Shaking him to wake up I noticed his dark skin looked ashy, confused I shook him again.

"Punch, Punch get up man, what's wrong?"

I was now panicking. He still didn't move, not even an inch. Thinking fast I grabbed his asthma pump while I held his head up.

Spraying the medicine in his mouth I lowered my head to his nose to see if he was breathing. I felt faint light breathing, and then he made an attempt to snuck in my air. I placed my oxygen mask on his face to help him breathe.

"Punch, stay right here, I gotta finish phase two!" I said when I felt like he was breathing better on his own.

Grabbing the AR's, I went to the top on the boat. It was a total of four workers along the boat.

Tat tat tat tat tat!

I shot each worker down then proceeded to the boat's control panel. Reaching in my pocket I grabbed the paper Punch gave me a few weeks prior and put in the new location coordinates. I placed the auto mode back on and went to get Punch.

"Nigga, I almost died in this stank ass bag!" Punch said as I walked back to where he was. He was still weak but was going to be ok.

Tossing the workers bodies overboard but not before searching their bodies. I took each of their passports, phones, and whatever cash I found. Punch was still trying to calm his breathing, so I made sure every I was dotted for us both. Grabbing my backpack, I grabbed the lunch my mother fixed us before I left.

"Phase two is completed!" I said to Punch as I handed him a phone I took from the guards. "We rich my brudda!" I said just as we saw the skyline of Miami a few hours later. "Call your uncle and tell him, we made it." I said in total awe of the beautiful sight before us.

Fast forward a year after we jacked the boat, Punch and I became not only rich, but powerful. Punch's uncle is the mayor of Miami, and he was just as money hungry as us. With his protection, and our drugs and pipeline for pure, uncut cocaine we reign supreme.

With more money than I can ever spend, I longed for something I didn't know I wanted. Don't get it twisted, I probably fucked every bad bitch in Miami. My name ring like an alarm clock at midnight, but I was no fool, they wanted me for clout.

I's been fucking with this chick Ayana on and off for two years. Shawty is bad as fuck, banging ass body, gorgeous face, A1 pussy, and fire ass head. She just doesn't want shit out of life though. She has no ambition at all. Shit, I gave the bitch ample enough time to show me what she's made of. All she wants to do is gossip on the phone with her hood rat ass friends, shop, and complain about what the fuck I'm doing in my spare time.

At first, I really thought she was the one. She had me fooled because she was doing her thing with promoting parties out here. When we first met, I asked her what she wanted to do, and told me, she planned on making her business bigger and better. My dick would brick up when I called for some neck and she hit me with the, "Bae I'm rack racing, give me a few. I got you though, daddy!"

I mean she was doing what the next bitch wasn't, giving me a chase.

All that shit went out the window when we started rocking heavy. I moved her in a mini mansion in Bel Bay and spoiled her rotten. I wouldn't say I loved her, but I had feelings for her. I even invested in her dream business I heard her talk about so many times. I had yet to see anything happen with that shit. I gave the bitch a hundred bands to start her off. Imagine how pissed I was when I pulled up to her spot and saw a brand-new McLaren in the driveway two days later. I don't give a fuck about the money, because I'm rich as fuck, but I need a shawty that's going to help clean this money up.

I never even asked her about the business again, I just sat back and watched. Fast forward to a year later and the bitch hasn't done anything with the business at all. I'm spending less and less time with her and she has the audacity to ask me why? I mean we aren't in a relationship r anything so I don't know how she figured she could ask me anything.

I mean she cooks, cleans, and fuck a nigga on demand but I need more than that. I could ride down South Beach and pick up any shawty to do that. I remember saying that to her once, while we were in a little disagreement. The bitch actually fixed her mouth to say, "Well, she could never suck your dick like I can," Rolling her neck around like a fucking bobblehead.

I decided at that very moment, I would never wife her in my life. If all she can offer on her resume is sucking dick, she's a cluck. I'm really not in the business of training a bitch on anything, so it is what it is. I just stick around for now because shawty really has some power neck.

******Present Day******

YAYO

I knocked on the door to the guestroom Kasha was staying in.

"Open it!" I heard her sexy ass call out.

Walking in, I had to adjust my dick because shawty was raw as fuck. Baby girl had on an all-white liquid looking two-piece tube top and skirt that hugged every curve, along with white Louboutin's. I forgot what the fuck I came in this room for, but shit, now I wanted to fuck.

"I'm almost ready for the meeting with your crew, did you need something?" She asked, knocking me out my trance.

"Damn, baby girl you bad as fuck," I let her know while staring in her eyes.

Walking over to me, she grabbed my dick with a smirk.

"Is that right, Yayo?" she hissed. That had me smirking back because this thick ass log caught her by surprise. I could tell because she jerked her hand back fast.

"Fuck yeah," I let roll off my tongue.

"Well, thank you, sir," she said just above a whisper, all shy like.

I guess this dick had her scared. I knew her type though; she's used to bossing up on niggas. But when, YES WHEN, I put this dick in her life, I'll show her who's boss around this mother fucker. I always get what the fuck I want, and I want Ms. Kasha something terrible. She had her hair pulled up in a bun so, I went to stroke her face, again an electric shock went through my body.

Why the fuck this keep happening? Is this a sign? If so, I'm going to find out. This is the second time it happened since she's been here.

The thing that really intrigued me is her eye contact, it's like she looks through you. It doesn't help that her eyes are a beautiful shade of light hazel. I find myself getting nervous when she stares at me, and I'm not the type of man to be intimidated.

I've killed more people than I care to admit. So, I'm definitely not scared of anything. It's just something about shawty though, I can't explain it.

Just know shit is about to get real, because I'm going to shoot my shot.

"Come on, future wife," I said on the slick.

Taking another look at shawty had me wanting to fuck her right here. In due time, I'm going to train her ass to be my queen though.

"Nigga, bring your ass on, we have money to make," she said, turning me on even more.

Watching her twist her sexy ass down the stairs and to the door, I fell in love. Not literally, because I'm a thug, but shit I wanted her ass.

I set the meeting up at a strip joint my partner owned called, The Office. I had all the coke Auntie and The Family needs, but they will be needing a route. So, I'm going to introduce wifey to my nigga LT and get that situated.

After helping her get into my custom chrome Bugatti Chiron, I smashed to the club. We made small talk on the way there, but I could tell she was in her boss lady zone.

Pulling up, I saw all the bucket bitches eyeing my whip. Pulling up to the front, I let my nigga Tone park my whip.

"Come on sweetheart," I said guiding her by her small waist.

Inside was a zoovie for real, it was a lot of fake ass everywhere. Paying attention to Kasha, I noticed she seem content and comfortable. Every once in a while, I see her adjust her skirt over her bullet wound, but other than that she was cooling. "We can get straight to business now, or we can chill for a few." I said in her ear so she could hear me above the music.

"Nah, let's get to business then chill after.", she replied back.

"Cool," I said leading her to LT's office.

"Nigga, your ass still ugly as fuck!" I said to LT as soon as I walked in.

"Aw nigga fuck you, whicho crispy black ass." He took a jab at me back.

Sharing a laugh, we shook hands.

"Well, damn who's the sexy ass queen?" he asked staring at Kasha like she was a whole meal. Wondering how she would handle it, I let her reply.

"I can be either a beautiful dream or a beautiful nightmare. That depends on you, Yayo says you can get my shipment to me. Care to breakdown numbers, or I have to pretend to like you?" She let him know with a sexy smirk on her face.

Low-key I was fist pumping like "Der go my bitch," but I just kept my straight face.

"DAMN, shawty don't play, huh? Yea shawty, I'm the man for the job. Have a seat while I breakdown this master plan for you." LT got into business mode.

Thirty minutes later the business part was done, and now I wanted to have a good time.

"You trying to fuck with the kid, and let me show you how we do in Miami?" I asked Kasha with a toothless smile.

"Yeah, daddy, show me how you get it," she teased back.

Ordering two bottles of Ace of Shade we proceeded to get fucking lit. After getting our bottles we went into VIP, with all the stripper hoes following us.

"I'm about to get some ones, let's cut up." Kasha let me know.

All of a sudden, I heard the DJ cut the music off and I was confused.

"I don't know who shawty is that just ordered ten thousand for VIP but shit about to get popping in this bitch!" I heard DJ Major Boi shout through the microphone. Shaking my head, I knew it was Kasha's ass. Stepping back into the booth she sat on my lap.

"I'm going to take over your city, lil nigga", she said as the bottle girl came with the ones.

"Nah, baby girl. You don't have to do that; the city is mine. Since you're going to be mine soon its yours too." I bit my bottom lip.

Kasha Diaz

By this time all the dancers were in our section. Kasha stood up and grabbed a bundle of ones. She went to the balcony and threw them in the crowd, making a money shower. I cackled a little because some of the dancers went running back into the crowd to pick them up. Taking her seat back on my lap she began dancing as Hood Celebrity's *Walking Trophy* boom through the club. Twerking her ass still sitting on me, she moved to the rhythm.

My eyes are following her as her body move calculatingly. She was in her zone grinding until she placed her hand over her bullet wound. Wincing in pain she sat down and our eyes connect.

"You ok?" I damn near yelped.

"I'm fine, I'll take my medicine when we get back, until then can you be that for me?" she cooed.

"What, your medicine?" I challenged. Smirking and shaking her head yes seductively.

Damn, shawty was fucking up my head already.

*****

KASHA

I don't know what had gotten into me but Yayo was looking sexier by the minute. It was always business over everything with me, so now that it was handled, my attention was on him. I was happy that I added a million dollars more a month of product to the family's workload. LT gave me his word that he would get Yayo's product to me safety every month. I decided that we could celebrate a little in this popping ass club.

I almost forgot a bitch had a bullet wound under this latex for a second. Well, until I whined my ass too hard and felt a sharp pain in my stomach. I sat my ass down with the quickness that shit hurt for real. Yayo's entire demeanor changed when I clutched my stomach, the nigga was making sure I was good though. The Ace of Spade had a bitch lit and this sexy ass nigga was gassing me. Looking around I noticed all the dancers with the stank face watching me. All the while lusting and begging for his attention.

These bitches need to back up off my man... Wait, what the fuck I'm even thinking. See, this drink and pain medicine have me tripping off this nigga, and he's not even mine. Let me just enjoy the night! I thought signaling a dancer over. She was the only one that was really working the VIP, the others just sat around, eye fucking Yayo and I.

Making her way to us she leaned over and smile. Taking notice that her body isn't or at least didn't look fake I gave her a head nod. She's was the color of sand, with calming grey eyes. Taller than I am especially with her dancer shoes on, she's beautiful.

"You guys are a beautiful couple, I'm Cash. Can I dance for y'all?" she asked sweetly.

"Hey Cash, I'm the number one Kash in here. Yes, show us a good time," I joked.

Taking a seat next to Yayo I was ready to see her in action. Looking over to him I could see his dick was hard as a brick of cocaine. Taking in the view, we ended up in another stare-down.

"Here have some fun Ya!" I say to Yayo handing him a bundle of money.

Taking a step back after I poured another drink for the three of us. I watched as the dancer snaked her body in front of Yayo, while he watched, but never touched her. Every so often he would flick money in the air, and it flew in the air. She was a very skillful dancer; she didn't just twerk like they normally did. She did tricks standing up on one leg while she mouthed the words to the songs, looking down at him. She was so entertaining I decided I wanted to join in on the fun, so I did. Yayo and I started going dollar for dollar tipping her as she continued to do her thing. Ten songs later, we had made the dancer 20 thousand dollars richer.

The other dancers looked on as if they were waiting their chance but the way Yayo was sitting next to me looking like a meal, they would be waiting.

"Let's go, boo," I said in his ear as I threw our last bundle of ones to the sideline dancers.

Standing, I thanked the danced who knew as Renni Rucci. My stomach wound had started back hurting, but I had such a great time, I didn't complain. We made to Yayo's car and he helped me. I had to let him even if I didn't want to, the pain was full blown by this time. We talked a little as the smooth voice of 6lack played in the background.

"So, what you thought about the business deal back there?" Yayo asked. I knew he was trying to take my mind off my pain, and I appreciated it.

"Well, I don't do any faking. If I felt I was bull shit, we were going to be in a shootout, my nigga." I shrugged letting him know. We both laughed but I was dead ass serious, he will find out soon enough. I'm really about my money, and I'm really with all the bullshit, if I need to be.

"That dude in the club that night, back in Charleston, is that your man?" he questioned. I was surprised he remembered it because she much had happened since I clearly forgot.

"My ex. That was actually the night I decided I was over him. I mean, I knew I was but I officially ended things." I filled him in. I wasn't going to ask he was single because I really didn't care. I'm attracted to him like crazy, but I'm not ready for another relationship.

"You sent my bottle back that night. Hurt a nigga's feeling, shit," she joked as we pulled into his estate.

"That cheap ass bottle! Who even drinks that shit?" I spat back as I let out a small laugh, since it hurt my belly to laugh hard.

"It was all they haddddd," he replied as he scooped me out of the car and walked with me in his hands.

I was happy Product decided to handle his own task for tonight. He knew a few goons out this way, so he had meeting to get them on our team out here. Yayo laid me against the bed in the room I would occupy while I was at his home. He left and grabbed me a water for me to take my pain medicine. I quickly took the three pills he gave me and laid back, while he ran me a bath.

"It's going to sting a bit but I think you should wash your wound, it will also relax your body, gangsta."

He called to me from the bathroom that was connected to the room. I carefully peeled myself out of the two piece, and almost passed out from the pain. I stood in only my white thong while I used my hands to cover my breast as best I could. Yayo eyes bucked out of his head when he returned to the room, but with concern. Tears fell from eyes as I limped towards the bathroom.

"Babe, come on," he responded breathlessly ordered.

We made it to the tub and fear halted me to try to step inside of it. Yayo had some type of herbs in the water and it smelled woody.

"It's an herb bath, the yarrow and limestone power with help speed up the healing process. My mother taught me this remedy years ago," He explained.

Even though the pain was unbearable, I still felt the butterflies swarm inside of me. He carefully picks me up and placed me inside, with my thong still on. As he turns to leave, I stopped him before he could.

"Yayo, thank you. Please don't think I'm some weak ass bitch, because I cried," I said to his back.

"I could never see you as weak. You're a boss." He threw over his shoulder as he left out of the room.

The warm water and the mixture of drug soon relaxed me enough that the pain subsided. Every so often Yayo would pop his head in and ask if I was cool. He even warmed the water up twice. Soon after he came in with gloves on and washed my wound careful with some other herbs. It hurt a little but it also soothed it at the same time. After he was done, he wrapped it this cloth that was silk like, but still was a bandage. I made it in the room with his help and he had a full meal spread out for us. I know I'm a thug but he really was bringing the girlish part of me, and I liked it.

"Eat, so you can get your strength, Kash," he again ordered.

For the first time I didn't have to tell a guy what to do, he just took control. I've never had that with Shawn's ass, I would have to baby step his ass through everything. My pussy was wetter than a Seattle rainy night at this point. We ate and laughed at Martin on the huge TV hinged to the wall in front of the bed for an hour. The drugs took over my body and soon I was out like a light.

A few hours later I woke up and looked over to my right at a sleeping, Yayo. He was laying on his back with one arm across his face and the other by his side. He was turned towards me and looked sexy even with his dreads all over his face and head. His full lips peeped through his hair and I wanted to kiss them. The light from the TV shone just enough for me to view this beautiful creature next to me. "It's time to take your meds again, Kasha." He whispered startling me. Reaching over he handed me my concoction, and went back to sleep, after I took it.

This man is going to be the death of me. I thought to myself as I scooted closer to him. His back was now to me, so I threw my arm around him and fell back into my blissful slumber. That night we took turns flipping over and holding each other, it came so naturally.

"WHAT THE FUCK?" Product shouted the next morning.

Jolting Yayo and I out of our sleep.

The gangsta part of us made us quickly grab our weapons that was tucked under our pillows. My eyes landed on my cousin and I knew he was about to be on some other shit.

"Why is this nigga in the bed with you Kasha?" Product spat dangerously as the fire danced between both, Yayo and me.

"After the meeting, her gunshot wound started to bother her. She was getting an infection, so I nursed and changed it. I stayed with her all night to make sure she was good," Yayo coldly responded back to Product. They got into this deadly stare down that shook my body.

These niggas are finna kill each other, I thought with panic drumming inside of me.

Product abruptly turned and stormed out of the room. My cousin had always been protective over me, so this wasn't a shock. At some point though he has to realize I'm a grown ass woman, and he had to chill.

"Let me go talk to this nigga," I said wiggling off the bed slowly.

Walking to the room Pee chose, I lightly tapped on the door. I didn't wait for him to respond as I opened it.

"Pee, what was that back there? You know I'm grown, right? BUT nothing happened with us at all. I thought I was dying, so he took care of me, SIMPLE!" I harshly yelled at him. I was now pissed because this nigga was about to kill Yayo, and I didn't even get the dick, yet. The scowl on his face confirmed my thoughts, and I knew shit was bad. Moments seemed to pass behind her opened his mouth to talk.

"You're right, Kash. You're grown and I have to remember you're not the girl I had to protect from the boys, all those years ago. My bad baby girl. I was about to kill both y'all asses," he uttered, throwing in a joke at the end for his apology. Walking over he hugged me and just like that, he was back to being my favorite cousin.

"Nigga, I almost shot you! The fuck you're talking about," I clowned as we hugged. "I'm going to freshen up, cause a nigga got me fussing with the morning breath and shit." I continued as I walked out of the room. I shook my head at Product's antics and ended passing Yayo going to room.

"I'm sorry about that Ya. Everything is good." I called out to his back, loud enough for him hear. He didn't bother to respond or look back as he kept walking, slamming his bedroom.

Both these niggas are crazy as fuck. I said to myself as I let out a deep breathe. I would speak to Yayo after he calmed down some, for now I had more pressing issues.

Today, I had to meet with Product's Miami goons and lay down the law about how I wanted things ran. It's always stressful meeting new people in this business especially that I'm a woman. Men had issues when a bitch is their boss, and I always ending up killing a nigga. Hopefully, they fell in line, and no bodies are dropped, because I damn sure didn't mind smoking a nigga.

After taking care of my hygiene, I figured I would dress down today. Since I did a little too much last night with the heels and stuff. I opted for a short two piece, red and white jersey set. It was loose enough around my abdomen, but still squeezed my ass in the right way. I threw on my Jordan red and white Jordan concords, and made sure my juicy lips were red also. The custom nine-thousand-dollar bangle earrings and bracelets set give my country girl swag. Looking at myself in the mirror, I checked over my appearance, and was pleased.

Miami belongs to The Family now. I mouthed to myself in the mirror. I meant every word.

Chapter 10

AUNT DOT

"They say with big money comes even bigger problems." I thought to myself as I looked over the books in my office. According to my bank statements, along with the offshore accounts, I'm rich. I'm here to tell you though money ain't shit without my husband here with me. Oh, my bad, where's my manners, my name is Dotty.

Everyone around the hood calls me Aunt Dot though. I've been in the dope game since a jit. My father was a kingpin, may God rest his dope slanging soul. At the age of five I realized I was hood royalty, I asked for a pony and I got one. My papa spoiled me rotten, I was his princess. My mother was his queen and we had shit black people shouldn't have back then.

In Love with the Queen of SC

My momma was the most gorgeous woman I've ever seen. My papa was smitten over her. She wore diamond rings on every finger, and he wore real furs and drove expensive cars. My childhood memories are filled with love and happiness, until the ultimately demise of my parents. I remember it like it was yesterday.

****

I was playing with my toy china set with my sister little Keesha in our playroom. I could hear Marvin Gaye's "I Want You" playing from my parents' room. I snapped my fingers as I poured the coke soda I pretended was tea in my doll's cup.

"This my song!"

Keesha began dancing along to the music.

"Yesssss!" I said as I slapped hands with her. We both began to two steps like we've seen our parent do on countless occasions.

We were enjoying the song so much that we didn't notice our father at the doorway smiling.

"That's right, babies, get down!" my papa said joining us in the two-step session.

A moment later my mother was joining us, and we all were singing the words loud pretending to be a band. I had the brush up to my mouth like a mic, singing my heart out. At ten years old I didn't really know the meaning of the song, but I loved it anyway.

"Baby girl's, if a guy doesn't love and want you like this song, walk away!" Daddy yelled over the music, while he and my mom danced together lovely.

Popping my fingers, I spun around and giggled at my parents. At the moment daddy's henchman Rondell burst into our playroom.

"We have to go, NOW!" he roared. My parents prepared us for this day since I can remember, so my sister and I sprang into action.

Each room in our home was connected to the underground tunnel. We all rushed to the huge mirror near the closet. It was a secret door, Rondell opened it and we all filed in. The tunnel was dark until my papa hit the switch.

"Move fast, but quietly just as we practiced," he said. I should have been scared but we were drilled some many times about this it became second nature.

Following the trail like we hundreds of times before, we made our exit safely. The bulletproof Cadillac sat there waiting for us. Rondell hopped in the driver's seat, while papa and mama sat in back with us. No one said anything as we made our way to our granny's house.

Once we were there, papa got out of the car and went inside. Ten minutes later, all we heard were his screams. I watched with fear as my mama and Rondell jumped out of the car. Sitting on my knees I propped myself up too see what was going on.

"Stay right here, Keesha," I whispered to my younger sister.

Opening the heavy door, I ran to the porch behind the chaos. I saw papa and my mom standing over my grandma's dead body crying. It was blood on her face and favorite apron she always wore when cooking.

"Momma, I'm so sorry! I came to get you! THEY KILLED MY FUCKING MOMMA!" Papa screamed.

Creeping back on the porch then running back to the car with tearing in my eyes. I hurried back inside the car with my sister.

"What happened, Dottie? Why are you crying?" Keesha asked with tears now in her eyes.

"I don't know but I do know Papa is going to kill everybody in this town!" I said giving her a hug.

"Don't cry Keesha papa gonna make sure we are ok," I said drying our faces.

The door opened and Papa, Momma, and Rondell got back in and we pulled off. I looked over at my father and I swear I saw evil if it ever had a face. The tears were gone and they were replaced with a vicious scowl. Even to be as young as I was, I knew my Papa was a menace in them streets.

I grabbed his hand and looked straight ahead, and momma grabbed Keesha's. The entire ride no one said anything. Forty-five minutes later we pulled up to a house I never saw before. It was big and beautiful but not like ours we just left.

Getting out the car, we went inside, and my sister and I just went with the motions. We were taught to never question our parents, and that it could cost our lives. Momma took us upstairs and to a room. It was decorated with pink and yellow flowers and had toys like we had at home in it.

"Freshen up for dinner. I'm going to the store to get groceries," she said just above a whisper. I could tell she was sad and wanted to cry.

"Yes ma'am," Keesha and I said together.

Momma came over and hugged and kissed us both.

"I love you girls. You love me, right?" she asked this every night before bed.

"Yes ma'am. We love you momma!" we recited again together. She walked out and closed the door.

We both ran to the window after we heard Papa said he was coming to take her. Getting into a different Cadillac we watched as they got in the car.

"BOOOOOOOOOOOOOM" The car blew up and fire was all over the yard.

"NOOOOOO PAPA, MOMMA!" I screamed. Rondell ran to us before I got a chance to get to the car. He whisked us away, driving with a maniac. I watched as the car and house disappeared in the back window.

Chapter 11

Present Day

Shaking the vivid images of my parents from my head, I poured myself a shot of Bourbon, preparing to finish this war with Raul. The war is definitely already in full throttle, but I have plans to *kill the head and watch the body fall.*

Finishing off another shot I thumbed through *my little black book* of contacts, my husband and I both had one. I'm not sure what happened to his because it never surfaced after his death. Knowing my husband, it would someday, but as long as it didn't land in the wrong hands, like the FEDS, it was cool.

Flipping the pages, I saw the contact *Mula Until the World Blow*, I ran my finger along the written words.

Yeah, shit is about to get really crazy, I spoke to myself since I was alone.

Not thinking about it further I went to my safe and retrieved my secure phone that I had for the contact in the black book only.

"Mula Until the World Blow," I said once I heard the line stopped ringing. The phone disconnected and I knew the button had been pressed, and shit was about to get hectic.

Let the games begin, I thought as I broke the phone into two pieces and threw it in the trash compactor.

Thoughts of what would happen for the next few days crossed my mind. Once that call was placed it's not coming back from it, but my back is up against wall. I rather kill off every threat before I gave them to thought of harming anything around me, so I hope they are ready for the chaos I'm about to bring. Waltzing over to backer to my closet I prepared for my dick appointment that was within in the hour. After my husband's untimely death, I refused to give my heart to anyone except family, but I did have a soft spot for O'har. We had this understanding going on for four years now, but lately he's been asking a lot about if I'll settle down that surprisingly have me thinking about my life. O'har is also a street vet, but we never mixed our businesses together, we gave each other advice on things when we get into our smoking sessions but that's it. I guess that's the reason why he's always my first choice, things are just easy with him and he truly understands me.

"If you could any sexier, I'll probably be in trouble," I heard O'har's voice say behind me. As always, he's early and his voice alone sent me in a sexual bliss.

Turning towards him I took in the beautiful creature God himself took extra time on. His salt and pepper full beard graced his brown face. His bald head wasn't shiny, but it was smooth and with any flaws. His dark eyes ran along my curves while his thick, bushy eyebrows heighten as he watched me. His six-foot five frame leaned against the door with his long arms folded in front of him. I stared at his toned body that is chiseled to perfection under his black leather jacket and relaxed fitted jeans he wore, with equal lust in my eyes. We did this every time we encountered each other, the stare down, the sexual tension always brew until it spilled into the room we occupied.

"You're early as O'har, why you always catch me off guard?" I bashfully asked as I decided it would be pointless to try to change at this point.

Walking over to him I greeted him with a flick of my tongue across his thick lips that barely peeked out from under his bread. As powerful and manly as O'har was, I was his weakness and I knew it, secretly he's mine also, so everything we did came naturally. He grabbed my lips into his and we kissed our stressed away for a few moments before he stripped my top off, popping every button off my five thousand Louis Vuitton blouses.

In Love with the Queen of SC

O'har carried me into the master sweet as I planted kisses all over his neck. I started sucking on his Hershey skin and rubbing the tips of my fingers up and down his forearm. This man was so damn luscious! We always had a good time when he got in my bed, but I could tell that tonight was going to be different. The vibe was different.

O'har lit some candles and turned on *More* by Joe. It had been a long time since I had sex to slow jams. O'har was taking it back. He got my body oil and began to run me down, slowly. Not missing an inch of my beautiful body. He took extra time on my inner thighs and feet.

"I just want to make you feel good, baby. I want to be the one thing in your life that isn't about business. Let me be that," he said as he slowly worked his tongue up my leg and to my flower.

O'har was the master at pleasing me with them kisses down long. His tongue worked its magic all over my clit, lips and in and out of me. I tried to fight the urge to grind my body into his mouth. He must have known my thoughts because he used his thighs to hold me still by placing both palms on my inner thighs and tightly gripping them

"Don't run now," he whispered to me before he went in and devoured my center.

My whole body jumped and twitched as I fought to keep my composure. I was dripping wet by the time he finally got inside of me. He teased me at first, swirling the head around my entrance; clockwise and then counter clockwise. By then, Keith sweat was singing in my ear.

Wanna feel your precious trenches
Wrapped around me, oh so tightly

If I hadn't have gotten my tubes tide, we would have been making a baby that night.

"Stoooop teasing!" I moaned out.

He slowly slid inside of me and worked me for almost an hour. His strokes were so damn deep! I couldn't take the sensual aspect of it. This definitely wasn't a dick appointment. We were making love.

"So, you're at war, Dottie?" O'har asked with concern etched along his face and brows. We were passing a blunt between the two of us and while Aaliyah's *I Don't Wanna* song cooed in the background. I explained to him that our time would probably been limited for a while due to the beef I had with Raul. He was always protective over me and it made me feel good to know he wasn't just a fuck for him.

"O'har, don't worry babe. I've made the necessary steps to protect The Family, trust me," I said as I laid back into his strong arms. We were now inside my bedroom here at my compound alone, well beside the fifty-two-armed guards placed outside and inside. I didn't sleep on my safety being the queen pin I am in no way at all.

O'har pushed to blunt back into my direction and grabbed my chin, I waited for him to speak. I knew him so well from studying his ways every time we linked so I knew he was about to speak.

"D, I never told you this but I love you. I'm not saying this because I want to change the dynamic of our situation, I'm saying it because I mean it. I respect your hustle, and I've never tried to stop you with any of it. I have to be real though, when I met you this was your life and I watched you reign out here in this underworld. Shit, honestly, I think that's one of the many reasons that I love you, but Raul is a different arena babe. He has a lot of connection in our country baby and I don't like that you are having problems with him. With all of that being said, I know you aren't a slouch out here, so my words to you are, trust no one", O'har spilled as he never broke eye contact with me.

He spoke with so much passion that I felt his words penetrated my entire being. If I was being to myself this man is my soulmate but the idea of it made me feel like I was betraying my deceased husband, Jr. I kept my feelings to myself and just pretended like this man didn't dominate my mind, body, and soul. I took heed to his words as always but decided against speaking to him further. Instead I let my eyes speak to his spirit and allowed him to continue with his rant. Moments later he was pacing the room on his cellphone, going off to who I'm assuming is connected to Raul's camp. Yeah, well that's my wife so I have to pull my business until this situation in her favor!" O'har continued, surprising me. He snapped his phone closed and plopped down beside me, rubbing his full beard with his long fingers.

"Why would you turn against your plug of fifteen years for me, O'har?" I asked in utter shock. Not only did this man cut off his money supply, he told me he loved me for the first time. I made sure to watch his body language because I could tell it changed a bit.

"I'm not fucking with him until the beef is cleared up or he's dead. I've been plugged in for fifteen years, I have enough to retire for three lifetimes. What I won't get another chance at, is being your man. I know you're the way you are to protect yourself, but I will not let anyone hurt you, including me."

I let out a raggedy breath of air as I learn intensively to him spill his heart to me.

"I've been single for so long baby, I'm not even sure if I know how to be with you. Jr broke my heart in pieces and I can't spend another ten years gluing what a nigga broke. I can't lie though; I love you too. I'm just scared of you, baby." I expressed my feelings as best I could. I could tell he was waiting for the letdown "I'm willing to give you a chance O'har, I trust you."

I continued snaking my fingers with his as I spoke. His eyes lit up as he kissed me before I could anything else. That kiss solidified us, and I vowed from this point forward I would let him lead me to the street glory. Only problem we had at the moment, was I already made an undoable call, all hell was sure to break loose. I prayed he was ready for the ride, and that he showed me he was Mr. Right.

What a way to start a new relationship, sheesh! I thought to myself.

My ringing cellphone jarred me from my thoughts, and I answered quickly when I realized it was Kasha calling me. I hadn't heard from her since she made it to Miami, which wasn't strange because we never used phones to speak about business.

"Kasha, how are you holding up, baby girl?" I asked as soon as I answered, and the line connected.

"Well, I almost died from the pain from this damn bullet inside me. But I took a pregnancy test and I'm not pregnant," she said letting me know that the meeting went fine and without any problems.

"Aww, well maybe you can try again. Everything happens in due time, you know. Just keep me posted, I'm about to make an appointment to have the mowers cut the grass. Call me later, and take it easy, okay" I replied letting her know I made the phone call to wipe out our now enemy, Raul.

"I will," she said quickly before we disconnected the call. I was ecstatic that things went well in Miami with Kasha and Yayo. This was a major pivotal point in our organization.

Chapter 12

Kasha

A few weeks in Miami had paid off. Ram and Product were slowly setting up shop and getting our workers relocated. Aunt Dot was keeping tabs on the war between The Family and Raul. They had blown up three more stash spots. Lucky for us, we had thought ten steps ahead of them and moved everything to their designated backup spots. Like I said, we play checkers, not chess. We needed time to figure out a plan to get this dick out of our lives. With Raul dead, we could rule in plain sight without anyone against us. But until then, the focus was flooding Miami with our product and drying everything else out. And with Yayo by my side, it proved easier than I thought.

Kasha Diaz

Over the course of the time I and been in Miami, Yayo and I had become closer. When we weren't working and making sure things were in place, we were sitting up; separating stacks and talking over a blunt. He seemed to be all over me, but I was not letting my guard down, so easily. He was fine and my type, but a bitch like me couldn't sit back and let any nigga call the shots. It was hard enough being a woman in this game and trying to be taken seriously. Niggas always assumed because we had pussies, that they could just stick a dick in us and make us be quiet while they took over. That shit wasn't happening on my watch.

It was a cold wind blowing through Miami as I sat on the balcony of the hotel suite Yayo had rented for us by the beach. I sat naked; looking at the sun while it set and taking pool after pull from my blunt. Miami had some good Kush, but it wasn't close to what I was used to. Tomorrow we were set to meet some soldiers of Yayo's camp. I was interested to see how this nigga ram things. He seemed like a strong leader, but niggas never hold their ground like women do. I needed to make sure he knew that I wasn't handing him over my empire. He was helping me get Miami, but this shit was mines. I was about to be running everything, including his team and operation.

I took another hit when Yayo appeared behind me.

"Damn! How you gone expect me to be about business when you're standing in front of me like this?" Yayo joked as he stared me up and down.

I turned and gave him a smirk. I could see the print in his white basketball shorts and bit my bottom lip.

"Shit, I don't know. It's ass all over the map. Can you stay focused on your business? Or will these lil' thirsty bitches be your downfall?" I questioned him as I stepped to him; switching softly and letting him get a full view of what I was working with.

Yayo rubbed his chin and bit his bottom lip. "Listen, ma... No pussy will ever have me out here slipping. You can guarantee that," he spoke boldly.

I was now standing right in front of him with my titties pressed against his chest. Yayo was dangerous, and though I was heavy on business shit, I couldn't fight this attraction I had to his ass.

"Good answer," was all I said before he lifted me off the ground and wrapped my legs around his frame.

We looked each other in the eyes before I slipped my tongue in his mouth. He carried me back inside and to the bed. He lay me down, softly and began to run his tongue from my neck to my chest and down to my honey pot. Yayo slowly worked his tongue on every inch of my body. Before I knew it, I was begging him to fuck me. He smirked at me; feeling like for once, he had something I needed. He slowly slid his shorts off and pulled a condom out of his pockets. I made a mental note to ask him about that, later.

In Love with the Queen of SC

My trust was so fucked up and Yayo made me feel a way that no other man could. I started wondering why I wasn't good enough to get the dick, raw.

Was I not worthy of carrying his seed? Did he think I had something? Did he carry that condom because he knew I would give in? I couldn't focus on that right now. I needed some penetration.

Yayo slid inside of me and my eyes began to bug out of my head. This man was blessed in every way. He slowly worked his manhood into me and before long, we were in sync. He was breathing deep into my neck and I kept my walls clenched tight around him. I could feel the earth moving beneath me as he worked out every stressful knot I had. It was like he knew my body better than I did. I didn't want him to stop. I was so addicted to him; I didn't even want to get on top. I didn't want to risk him slipping out of me, not like that was even possible.

When he started going harder, I low-key wanted him to slow down. It was like I wanted this nigga to make love to me, but I couldn't have that. Everything was a power move to me. Even fucking. I quickly flipped the script on put him on his back. I sucked up the pain and began to grind my body on his frame. He began to hiss and cuss. I knew I had his as. Without skipping a beat, I turned around and let him watch my ass bounce as I jumped up and down on him. With one hand, he slapped my right cheek and that shit sounded like thunder in the room.

Unable to just let me shine, Yayo pushed me forward without falling out of me, placed me on my knees and kneeled behind me. With a death grip on my waist, Yayo began to fuck the living shit out of me.

I couldn't hold it in anymore and began to moan and holler.

"Say my name, queen. say it," he demanded.

I was determined not to give that nigga what he wanted, but I didn't know for how long I could contain myself. Yayo had me right where he wanted.

"Say it's mine," he grunted.

I gripped the sheets and felt defeated. This nigga was about to kill me. I couldn't help it or fight it any longer.

"Oooh... Ya...Yo.... It's yours..."

****

The next morning, we all met up for breakfast and took two black trucks to the meet up spot to get better acquainted with Yayo's team. Aunty Dot let me know that she would be coming in two weeks to meet them, but that we had a big shipment coming in. Product was leaving to head the delivery and make sure nothing was wrong. I would miss my cousin, but I trusted him. Plus, I needed Ran here. Me and Yayo may have smoothed out the bumpy parts of our arrangement, but I still couldn't be left alone in a place I was still getting used to by myself.

Ram and Yayo rode in one truck and Product and I took another. For the first time, I was actually felling nervous and I was afraid that it would show. These niggas didn't scare me, Yayo did. He had a hold on me that I couldn't understand not shake. I found myself getting stuck on stupid when he came in the room. I'm usually the enforcer, but Yayo's presence just demanded respect and attention. I felt like I was falling for him, and I didn't know how to handle that shit. I couldn't let him get that kind of hold on me, not now. We were still at war and we're in the process of taking over the 305. I couldn't jeopardize that shit for some feelings, *right?* I didn't know what was happening, but I found myself missing Yayo when he was out of my sight.

That car ride down to his warehouse felt like it was taking hours. I had to keep an eye on their truck, as if I was afraid it was going to just disappear into thin air and that I wouldn't see him, again. Shit wasn't making sense at all and I needed to get a grip. I couldn't show weakness in front of some new niggas. I didn't need them challenging my power and going behind my back to Yayo. It's hard running shit as a woman and I didn't need these niggas thinking I was another piece of pussy fucking their boss. I was the fucking boss around this bitch.

I mentally prepared myself to get into boss bitch mood. I lowered my Chanel glasses over my eyes and checked to made sure my gun was tucked and ready. We followed behind Yayo's truck into a dark underground parking garage. We stopped right in front of a straight line of men in all black with clean cut faces and either neat dreads or freshly shaven heads. All of these niggas looked on point and crispy as fuck. When Yayo stepped out, all of their attention was on him. Ram got out and meet Product and I where we stood.

Yayo walked up to me and whispered in my ear. "You have the floor mats. This is your operation. Let it be known."

I had to admit; I was caught off guard. I thought he would at least address these niggas or introduce me or something. But he didn't. I got my grip and stepped to the front of the line and looked each one of them up and down. I took my glasses off so we could look each other in the eye. I knew the integrity of anyone by looking them in their eyes. I wanted to see who's as loyal and who was too loyal. Any nigga that I felt was out of line, would have to go. About this wasn't like back home. These niggas had Product, Ram and I out numbered. I knew if I shot one, we were all about to get shot. I was going to have to take notes of who could and couldn't stay around and tell Yayo. The thought of someone else having the overall button besides me made me sick. And the fact that that person was a man, was even worse. But, in that moment, I had to do what I had to do.

"Listen. I don't give a fuck who you may think I am or how you may view me. The bottom line is this; I'm about to be the Queen Pen of Miami. We got a big ass shipment coming thru in a few days. That's more drugs than any of y'all have ever seen in your whole lives. Weapons too. There are gonna be a lot of thirsty and hating ass muthafuckas who are going to try to come shut shit down and I won't be having any of that. Anyone that I suspect is moving funny, is getting gunned down with no remorse."

I stopped in front of the of one guy who had an eye tattooed between his eyes. He wouldn't look me in my eyes and that told me all I needed to know. I took a mental picture of his face to bring up to Yayo.

"And anyone I feel I can't trust will...."

Pop! Pop! Pop!

The entire room stayed still except for Ram, Product and I, we had hit the floor. We looked up and searched around and were confused as to why the rest of the team were standing still and unbothered. It wasn't until I noticed the same dude, I was taking a picture of in my head was now dead in front of me that I finally started searching for who had pulled the trigger. I turned and seen Yayo lowered his weapon and nodded.

"Finish what you were saying, Queen," he said.

"Is getting a toe tag…" I finally spat out.

"Now, Yayo spoke very highly of y'all. But I'll let your actions determine how true all of that is. As y'all will be finding out, I don't play about shit. Ram will be giving everyone their assignments, getting contact information and checking out y'all spots. We take care of all our family. So long as y'all don't step out of the lines, y'all are now a part of the family. My men will be marching down Ocean Drive as soon as the shipment has docked and the layout has been made."

After a while, the stuff was loaded into a black bag and taken to the ocean to be made into fish food. I opted to ride back with Yayo because I had so many fucking questions, but he turned me down. He said he and Ram wanted to go look at the trap spots and I needed to get Product to the airport. I was pissed, but I understood.

I dropped Product off and hugged him tight. I knew he was going to be okay, but I couldn't help hugging him as if it would be my also time doing so. I sat I the parking lot for an hour after his plane took off and watched the sun go down. My mind was racing, and I needed someone to help me make sense of the shit. I picked up my phone off the back seat and dialed aunty Dot. She hurried and picked up on the first ring.

"Niece, are you okay? Is something wrong?" she asked. I could hear the worry in her voice.

"What? Nah Aunty. Everything is fine," I said dryly.

"It's don't sound fine. Do I need to hurry up down there?" She raised her eyebrow.

I could hear a man's voice in the background asking her who I was, and did I need help. What took me out was hearing her say, *"No babe. It's just Kasha. Remember I told you the kids are setting up shop in Miami."* I cocked my neck back and stared at my phone in confusion. My uncle died years ago. So, who the fuck was she talking to about me like they knew me? And calling them *babe*?

"Aunty, who the fuck is that?" I spat into the phone. I could hear her walking into another room. "Aunty?" I hollered.

"Girl, hold on," she giggled into the phone.

I was so confused. I never heard my ruthless aunty sound like some damn schoolgirl before.

Damn, how long had I been gone?

"Niece, That's O' har. We together now. He let go of his connect with Raul just for me. I haven't felt like this since your uncle."

She kept going on and on about O'har and I couldn't help but laugh. Here she was; my ruthless boss ass aunty who cut off heads and shit, gushing over a nigga. I never thought I would see the day. It was like she was showing me what Yayo and I could be if I just let him in.

"So, aunty, how does this work with you being who you are? I mean, aren't you scared of losing control?" I asked.

"Listen baby, sometimes it's lonely being a cold-hearted ass bitch all of the time. Ain't no nigga taking my pedestal. But, it's nothing wrong with having somebody to take your mind off shit. This world gets cold and lonely and everybody needs somebody. It doesn't make you weak."

Hearing her say that was all I needed. She told me she would be booking her flight soon and that she loved me very much.

When we got off of the phone, I got this uneven feeling that I just couldn't shake, but I ignored it. I directed the driver to take me back to Yayo's. When I got in, he and Ram and a few other dudes were playing 2K. I stood in the doorway and watched from a distance. I wondered what it would be like to come home to the same loyal nigga every day. I imagined the other guys were our sons. It was a moment to take in and almost made me forget about our reality. Yayo saw me from the corner of his eye and flashed me a smile. I smiled back and headed up stairs to my room. I undressed and got in the shower. I was a mess of feelings and fear. I was at war and didn't have time for this.

What did this shit really mean?

When I got out, I dried off and put a robe over my naked body. When I woke into the room, Yayo was sitting on the corner of the bed with a blunt between his fingers.

"I thought you could use this after the day you just had," he said as he sparked it up.

I smiled and sat next to him. I waited until I knew we were both feeling it before I started asking my questions.

"So, what was that about today?" I asked, unable to figure out how to ask why he popped one of his own.

Yayo laughed and hit the blunt. "Simple. You didn't trust him. I could tell by the way he didn't look you in the eyes that he wasn't going to take you seriously. I don't want them niggas thinking they can go around you. I said this is your operation. And if they fuck with me, they need to fuck with you. Or no they will get laid down and K won't be there to save them," he said.

"So, you are saying I can toe tag any of them niggas if I don't trust them without coming to you?

You willing to let me murder your soldiers without running it down by you?" I asked in a serious tone.

Yayo turned to face me and look me in the eyes so I know that he was being honest. "You do what you gotta do. I got your back. But you don't need me to demand respect. You had shit popping in your city. You're in mine now. And I'm tryna make this ours."

I felt more comfortable and safer with Yayo than I had in the beginning. He was treating me like a Queen and the boss that I was. He was also showing me he was loyal, and I liked that.

"So, what was with the condom shit last night?" my thoughts finally came out.

Yayo laughed and handed me the blunt. "Oh, you mad because you couldn't feel it for real?"

We both began to laugh. I playfully punched him. He pulled me onto his lap and began to kiss on my neck.

"We are at war, aa. I don't want to knock you off your game. I wouldn't do anything to tarnish your rep. That includes getting you pregnant. Don't get me wrong, we would make some beautiful babies. But I don't want you to be seen as the typical hood bitch who falls victim to *the D*. I care about you in every way that a person could care."

I lowered my head on Yayo's shoulder and for the first time since I was a little girl, I felt safe. I felt like I could be open and vulnerable with him. I imagined us with little chocolate babies running around. That wasn't our reality, right now. But I was starting to wonder if it ever could be. If we could ever be just two regular people in love.

Yayo slowly began to kiss me and I felt a shock run over my body. I lay on my back as he began to kiss me all over. He looked me in my eyes and told me that he loved me. I felt a tear coming down the side of my face. I was scared as fuck, but I believed him. That night, we didn't just fuck. We made love.

The next morning, we lay in the dark; naked and wrapped around each other. Product shot me a text to let me know that he had made it safely and he would let me know when the shipment was en route. I looked at Yayo as he smiled at me.

"You ever think of what it would be like if we weren't in the line of work that we are in?" I asked, half afraid of his response.

"Before I met you, nah... I knew I never wanted to work for anyone or make another muthafucka rich ever again," he said.

I felt that shit. I couldn't be one of them paper pushing muthafuckas in a cubical; all dolled up to sit behind a desk and answer a fucking phone. I also couldn't be no stay at home bitch. I was a breadwinner. I loved the fell of money I had worked for in my hands. I loved giving commands and being at the head of the table. I couldn't imagine giving it all up. Not even for a second.

That night, we decided to step out. With my cousin on the move with the shipment, our soldiers heading out and Yayo's team falling in line and giving Ram all of the info, he needed, it felt like a good time to fall into the night life and make my presence feel known. Plus, I was dying to show Yayo off to these Miami bitches. I was sure he had fucked a few bad ones before me, but it was important for them bitches to know that they would never have him like I have him.

We were matching like twins that night. We were wearing creme white outfits and rose gold jewelry to accent everything. We took about a thousand photos just to find the right one for each other's contact photos. I'm not gone lie; we were acting hella goody. Acting as if we weren't running a multimillion-dollar drug ring. As though we both didn't have blood on our hands. As if we were who we were. For a second, I must admit, the shit felt great.

We arrived at a new strip club called Tarzan. The women in here looked hella exotic. We sat in V.I.P., *of course*. It only took a few shots for Ram to start feeling the effects and find himself out on the floor with some bad bitches. I couldn't help but laugh watching him have them chicks dance on him like he was the man. It was a different time in our lives. Any other time, this wouldn't be allowed. We couldn't get caught slipping'. But hey, it was a celebration.

Yayo and I stayed together and enjoyed each other's company. Every now and again, I would let some stripper come over and dance for us. I knew Yayo liked my wild side. I knew that shit turned him on. I could feel Yayo grabbing on my ass and giving me a smirk. I knew tonight was about to be lit.

*****

Yayo

Kasha was looking like the baddest bitch alive tonight. I couldn't keep my hands off her. I could see all these niggas in here eyeing her, but she was mine. I never felt this way about any woman, before. Kasha was different than any other chick I had ever been with. She was driven. She didn't need me, but she wanted me and that was saying some shit. I could see us in this for the long run on some Bonnie and Clyde type of shit. If I had to share my empire with anybody, I was proud to say it was her.

The liquor was setting into my system and I could barely keep my dick down while watching these dancers play with Kasha. I wanted her right there and then. I started touching on her to let it know it was real. She gave me a smirk and whispered in my ear to meet her in the bathroom. I watched as she switched from our section towards the lady's room. I polished off the last of the bottle and started to make my way through the crowd when u heard a familiar voice creep up on me.

"So, I gotta come to the strip club to see my man, now?" Ayana laughed at me as I turned to take her in. She was clearly drunk and tripping all over herself. The shit was embarrassing.

"I don't know. You'd have to ask that nigga," I tried to walk off because I was not her nigga.

Ayana reached out and grabbed me, which caught me off guard to the point I almost reached for that thang.

"Now come on, baby. Don't be like that. You know you miss me," she said as she tried to look seductive.

I laughed and shook my head at her. "Nah. from the looks of it, you missed me. Now if you'll excuse me."

I started to walk around het towards the bathroom. I couldn't believe her ass was following behind me. I knew if Kasha saw her, that was going to be both of our asses, but she wouldn't stop following me.

"Oh, what? You here with another bitch, Yayo? That's what we doing? Does that bitch know about me? I hope she know she gotta share!" Ayana shrieked behind me. She was making too much noise and causing a scene. I didn't need this shit right now.

I turned and got all up in her face so only she could hear me. "Listen, Ayana. You're causing a fucking scene, and I don't have time for this shit right now. You're drunk. Take yo' drunk ass home and I'll hit yo' ass up, later." I had to tell her ass something.

I didn't have time for Kasha to come out and see her following me and spilling our business.

Ayana rolled her eyes and licked her lips at me. "Alright, nigga. But if I don't hear from you, I'm coming to yo' crib. I told you. Ain't no bitch taking my spot," and with that, she turned and started to head for the exit.

I shook my head and ran my hand across my face. I really didn't have time for her delusional ass. I was pissed off and over this whole night. I just wanted to go home. I pulled my phone out to text Kasha to meet me at the car before I tipped the bartender who had been serving us all night and headed out. Ayana was going to have to be dealt with. I didn't love her; never had and never would. I wasn't about to let nothing stop me and Kasha from our missions; not Raul, not the Feds and most certainly not Ayana.

*****

Kasha

I read over Yayo's message and began to laugh. I walked away from the bathroom area and back to VIP. He may have been ready to leave, but I wasn't. I still wanted to drink and show off my body. I was feeling' Miami's nightlife and after that exchange I just watched between him and some random bitch, I really was in no rush to head back to the house with him. So, I went back up to VIP where Ram was at with some baddies. I ordered us another Bottle and we started taking shots.

I waited twenty minutes before I finally let Yayo know he could leave, and I would get with him later. I knew he was going to feel some type of way and that was going to make two of us. From the way he was in her face, whispering, that shit let me know they had a past that went deeper than just fucking. That shit woke me up and made me realize I didn't know everything I probably needed to about this nigga and yet, here I was falling in love with his ass. I needed to step back before I started thinking too much and it turned into rage. I was here in Miami on business and it needed to stay that way. But for now, I was going to get lit.

A quarter after three, Ram and I were stumbling out of the club and into a luxury car service. I went to the house, but Ram decided to go with the two bitches he had been dry humping all night.

"Don't get caught up," I joked with him before the car pulled off.

I huffed hot air before I finally made my way into the house. I was not in the mood to argue with Yayo. The world was spinning beneath me and I just wanted to sleep. I walked into the house to find him sitting at the bottom of the stairs. He jumped up when he saw me.

"Kash, didn't you see me calling you. I been blowing your phone up!" he yelled.

I cocked my neck back at him like he had me twisted. We had only fucked a few times and now this nigga was yelling at me? He must have forgotten who the fuck he was dealing with. I puffed air and headed up the stairs.

"Whatever, nigga," I mumbled over my shoulder.

"Kash, wait. Something happened. Product is here. He's in the master suite. Some shit went down!" Yayo hollered at me, freezing me in my tracks.

My heart skipped a beat as I skipped two steps at a time and raced down the hall to the master bedroom. Inside, I found Product laid on the bed with nurses attending to him. He was broken, bruised and bloody. I had never seen my nigga look so fucked up. I instantly started to cry as I rush to his side.

"What the fuck happened?" I whimpered out to no one.

Yayo entered the room, out of breath.

"He got robbed, Kasha. Somebody snuck onto the boat and they took everything. They killed everyone. They beat Product almost to death and tossed him off the boat. He almost died till a fisherman found him and he had him bring him straight to me. They took everything!" Yayo spat out. My eyes got big as I held my cousin's hand.

"Cousin, who did this?" I cried out to him. He couldn't speak and I couldn't understand why.

"Save him!" I hollered out.

Yayo came and grabbed me and walked me out of the room as I continued to yell. "If he dies, you all die!"

Chapter 13

I must have smoked ten blunts to calm me down. I couldn't stand seeing my cousin all fucked up like that. Never in my life did I think someone could or would ever try us in this way.

Never...

Yayo ended up calling a doctor to come examine Product. The decision was made to put him in a medically induced coma to stop the pain he was feeling. My nigga had major internal bleeding, some cracked ribs, and the propeller of the boat had sliced his face. He was going to need cosmetic surgery to fix what had been done. In other words, my cousin was out.

What made things worse was that I could not get in contact with my aunty at all. I knew she would want to know about Product's condition. I wondered if she knew we had been robbed. I knew that this was no one but Raul, *but how*? It didn't make any sense. Nobody knew about our dealings down here in Miami and I knew Aunty would not let just anyone in on this. So, how the fuck did this shit happen?

I drove myself crazy for two days over this shit. I refused to leave Product's side for the most part. I wasn't eating or sleeping. I was just calling my aunty back to back.

After the third day, my exhaustion got the best me and I needed to eat and get some sleep. So, Yayo set up cameras in Products room in the west wing of the house. We had guards all around, but we kept business going as usually. We hadn't told any of the workers we had been robbed. We had just established this union and couldn't let anything jeopardize this. I didn't need these niggas thinking I was weak because this happened on my watch and not Yayo's. I had to remain cool in the front of them, but in all honesty, I was fucked up, mentally.

In Love with the Queen of SC

We sat on the master bedroom floor; Yayo, Ram and I trying to eat some pizza, but the vibe was just completely fucked up. Nobody said a word because no one knew what to say or how to fix this. Raul had to die, that much we knew.

But how do you kill a nigga you can't get close to? And how the fuck were we going to get out shit back? And where the fuck was Dottie?

Soon, Ram's phone began to go off. He looked at it and whatever he was looking at made him drop the piece of pizza he was babysitting in his hands.

"Fuck No!" he hollered.

Yayo jumped to his feet while I stayed on the floor, looking up at them both. I was so damn weak, physically. Yayo snatched the phone and his face turned completely pale.

"What is it?" I asked as I slowly tried to get up.

The two looked at each other for the answer.

"Ram give me your phone," I demanded.

Yayo shook his head. "Kasha, wait," he stated. The look on their faces were causing me to panic so

I grabbed the gun from off of the bed and pointed it at them.

"Give me the fucking phone!" I hollered.

Ram looked so afraid and I had never seen him look that way. He slowly handed me the phone and as the image got closer to me, I began to tremble and shake. I dropped the gun as my jaw dropped damn near to the floor. My eyes grew big and began to water up.

"Nuh… no…" I whispered. My eyes focused on the image before me, and I realized it was real. "Nooo!" I hollered out before dropping to the floor.

Yayo rushed and picked me up as I began to swing my body, wildly at the air.

"Nooo, you muthafuckas killed her...no!" I screamed out.

Yayo rocked me back and forth, trying to comfort me. I couldn't shake that image of my auntie's severed head on a medal rod. That would be an image that would haunt fucking dreams for the rest of my life.

"Son of a bitch. He gone die... you hear me? *He is going to fucking die.*"

******

Hours later, I had awakened after passing out. Yayo and Ram were sitting downstairs waiting for me. I walked like a zombie down the stairs; not looking at either one of them, and trying not to blink. Every time I did, I would see my auntie's head all bloody. I wouldn't be unseeing that shit any time soon.

I walked towards the front door and stopped in my tracks to face them. I looked up at the ceiling to continue my emotions.

"How's Product?" I asked them in a scratchy voice.

"He's still under. The doctors are done on him, however. They said he can wake up tomorrow. "Ram filled me in.

"Good. Don't wake him up. Yayo, tell them to keep him sedated. I don't want him waking up until this is all over." I demanded.

They both looked at each other, confused before looking back at me.

"Kasha, you can't just storm Raul's place and kill him," Ram said.

I nodded and sucked in air. "What's the word on the streets back home?" I asked him.

"Nothing. No one hasn't said anything about it. I was waiting for your own wake up so we could fill everyone in," Ram answered.

"We're not telling them anything. Whoever killed my aunty, knew her. She would have never let an *Opp* get that close enough to her to slit her fucking throat. Somebody has betrayed her. I'm going home in the morning to find out. I already booked a flight."

"How many of our soldiers are meeting you at the airport?" Ram asked me.

"None," I responded.

"Kasha, somebody assassinated your aunt and sent us the photos to prove it. That's a calling card. He's coming for you and now you want to go out, unprotected?" Yayo asked.

I laughed at him. "I don't expect you to understand. Ram, you're going to stay here and keep shit in line with Yayo. Once it's done, I be home. "

Without another word I headed back upstairs to pack. I could hear Yayo behind me asking Ram what the fuck was I thinking and why wouldn't I let my team know what was going on. I could hear Ram giving him my favorite answer.

"Because we play chess, nigga, not checkers."
*****

The flight home was an anxiety induced ride. I never thought I would be coming home on such fucked up terms, but I did what I had to do. Once I landed, I called O'har's phone and he picked up on the first ring.

"Who this?" his deep voice pierced my ear through the phone.

"Hey, *New Uncle*. This is Kasha. Aunty Dottie gave me your number so that I could call you if I couldn't get a hold of her. Good thing too because I'm in town and I need to get this morning from her, but she not answering her phone," I explained.

"Yeah, she hadn't been answering mine either. I'm going to go stop by her place. I can meet you over there with the spare key," he politely offered.

I accepted and told him I'd be there shortly.

A few hours later and my Lyft was dropping me off in front of the house I practically grew up in. My aunty Dottie had taken me under her wing and raised me as her own. I was like the daughter she had never had. I felt a wave of fear and pain rush over me as I stopped outside, waiting for O'har. The house looked different. Everything looked dark and felt dead. I couldn't shake the feeling and it was making me sick. I wanted so badly for my aunty to run outside and say something, anything to me. Even though I've seen the photo, I just couldn't bring myself to believe that my ace boon coo was really fucking gone. Aunty was too much for a fucking boss to be murdered that easily. The shit just wasn't adding up.

I snapped out of my thoughts when I heard a car pulling up in front of me. O'har jumped out looking clean and put together in a nice suit with a real Rolex on his wrist. He checked his surroundings, locked his car and walked up to me.

"Miss Kasha, it's so good to see you in person. your aunt would always talk about you. She was so proud of you," he said.

I nodded and smiled. "I wish she could show that by answering her damn phone instead of having me come all the way over here," I joked.

"Oh, you been busy?" O' har asked.

I shrugged my shoulders and said, "Something like that."

He pulled out the spare key and we walked towards the entrance. I could feel my heart skipping a beat a second as we slowly walked into the house and called out her name.

"Dottie... Dottie..."

No answer.

We slowly made our way towards her office and to the double doors in the back of the house. O'har took a deep breath before opening the door. As soon as the door opened, the foulest smell I had ever smelled invaded my nostrils. O' har quickly turned away and stormed back towards the foyer. I plugged my nose and swatted at the hundreds of flies that were in the room. My eyes bugged out of my head when I saw my auntie's body decaying and headless propped up in her favorite chair. I couldn't believe that my aunty as just left to fucking rot and be fly food like this. This shit was beyond disrespectful. She deserved so much fucking more than this.

The smell had finally gotten the better of me and I slowly backed out of the room and closed the doors. I rushed to the kitchen and began to vomit in the trash can. I was shaking so violently, that I began to cry and feel pain in my body. I quickly began to drink cold water from the faucet and gasp for air. I punch at the cabinets and tried to fight the urge to break down and cry. There was going to be a time for me to grieve, but right now was not that fucking time.

I walked into the foyer and found O'har pacing back and forth.

"Who would do something like this to her?" He was asking no one at all.

"Raul," I answered.

He spun his head towards me in shock.

"Raul did this. It's payback for Aunty cutting his wife's head off. He did this. And he will get his," I said out loud.

"Kasha, Raul is untouchable. How do you expect to get him when Dottie couldn't?" O'har asked.

I didn't answer him. I just pulled don't my phone and made a call. I let O' har know that Aunty was going to be cremated and that the police were not to be called. I told him I would keep in touch before ordering a Lyft and taking off. I lost it in the back of that car. I cried harder than I ever have. To tell you the truth, a part of me died in the back of that Lyft.

Kasha Diaz

I sat in my hotel suite and began to roll up when Ram hit my line. I let him know that Aunty was going to be cremated and brought back to Product. The break in his voice let me know that he was fucked up behind the truth. *We all would be.*

"Look, Kasha. I know this ain't the best time for this, but we got bigger problems right now," he said into the phone. I couldn't help but laugh at him.

"Yeah, I know. The boat is gone." I shook my head as I began to spark my blunt.

"Nah. Bigger. All our allies got that picture of Aunty. Raul put the fear in them. They all pulled out. The Jamaican's, the Gorillas, *everybody*. We on our own out here," Ram said.

I shook my head and tossed my blunt across the room. I of course couldn't believe this shit. Raul was sucking us dry and murdering off the ones we lived. We couldn't operate like this, and like my aunty before me, I wasn't about to bow down to him or nobody.

I got my head together and started running the plan down with Ram. It was time to end this shit. Before I hung up, I gave the order to keep Product sedated until I got home. I didn't need him waking up and finding out the news while U was gone. He was a wild card and would blow up the whole world behind his mother. Once we hung up, I picked up my blunt and let Mary fuck my Brian. I began to laugh and jab my finger in the air.

"You want a war, muthafucka?" I asked to nobody at all. "I'll give you a war!"

******

The next day, I picked up my Auntie's ashes from some of my men. I placed them in my bag and left them in the room. I had one of my goons, Beast, drive me to make my runs. I picked up what I needed and headed to Queens, New York. We had a house set up for occasions like this. Normally, I wouldn't opted to play this damn dirty, but business was business. Raul had crossed the line, and there was no going back after this.

I sent O'har the address to meet me so we could talk. He arrived just as the sun was about to start setting. I stood in the living room with a picture of Aunty Dot hanging above the fireplace. She looked like a damn queen and that's how I wanted everybody to remember him by. I kept my eyes on it as O'har walked into the house.

"Kasha, what's going on?" he asked in a frantic.

"Why are you out here in New York?" I looked at him with a blank face.

"Raul has sucked our allies away. He killed my aunty. I'm ready to end this war," I said as I kept my eyes on my auntie's photo.

"Kasha, you know he isn't going to let up without your head," O'har reminded me.

I laughed and nodded. "He has no choice if he wants his prize possession back "

I pointed to the room towards the back of the house. O'har's eyes got big as he slowly crept towards the door. He opened the door and quickly closed it.

"Kasha, have you lost your fucking mind?" he hollered.

"No. I've lost my money, my product, my allies, and my aunty. The time for respect and boundaries has died. If he wants his prize back, he'll back the fuck off," I said as walked away and signaled for him to leave.

A few hours later, Beast helped me load up and leave the house in Queens. We went back to aunty Dot's house and waited. Around two in the morning, I got that call.

"Yo Kasha, you were right about the house party in Queens. Raul's boys just couldn't help but crash the spot. But you know us, we got them lit."

My eyes in the sky filled me in. I shook my head before hanging up. Being right all the time was a bitch!

I sent Beast to get me Red Bull and had one of Dottie's nurses give me a shot of adrenaline. I needed to stay up. Around five in the morning, I got a call from a blocked number. I answered with the coldest tone.

"What?"

"Bitch! who the fuck does you think you are?" Raul spat into the phone with his thick accent.

"I'm the bitch who has your son. And if you want to see him, alive, you'll give me back my aunties head." I demanded.

The line went cold before Raul began to speak.

"Where are you?" he asked.

I laughed inti his ear as I felt the heat rise from my body. "You know how to find me, bitch ass!"

Click!

Chapter 14

There was only one line that my aunty would have never crossed when it came to this game, and that was involving innocent children. I never in a million years thought that I would be holding someone's child hostage and, believe me, this was the last thing I wanted to do. But, what other choices did I really have? Raul had forced my hand; killing my kin, stealing my product, and leaving my cousin to die. He had left me out of options and out of time.

Shit was moving too good in Miami for me to have to constantly be looking over our shoulders for the next attack. I couldn't live that way any longer. In addition to that, it wasn't as though once Raul got his son back that shit would just be good. He would have all of our heads. I had to do what was best for us, in the end. I just hoped that my aunt could forgive me.

What really took me out was how someone as evil and hated as Raul could still find time to get married and reproduce. It made me wonder about my future; if someone would ever be calling me mommy? It also made me think about Yayo and where we were at. I still couldn't shake the visual of seeing him conversing with some other bitch. I knew he had a whole show going before I got to the 305, but what if it wasn't over? I had enough of exes and shit with my own ex and having watched all the women in my life go through it with men. I would be damned if I let Yayo do as he pleased on me. I wasn't about to be one of these weak bitches still staying with a nigga after he had violated and disrespected me just because *I loved his ass*.

In the end, I knew I would have to confront him about the shit, eventually. The fuckery duo reality was that if I couldn't accept what he told me, I been we couldn't continue our operation together. I also knew that killing him would start a whole 'notha war that I didn't need. But, for now I would just have to deal with that on another date…

*****

O'har

I couldn't believe I was back in the mix between Dottie's family and Raul. I thought when it came out that Dottie was dead, her niece would go into hiding, and I could finally be done with the game. I was an old cat and these new niggas didn't respect moral code. That was further proven when Kasha showed me, she had kidnapped Raul's Jr. *What the fuck was she trying to pull?* And now here I was, in the middle playing delivery man. I was on the verge of rebranding myself and walking away from the drug and sex game. And here they were, dragging me back in. *But what else could I do? Say no to Raul?* I wasn't stupid. Not by far. So, I had this one last drop to make, an exchange.

Raul told me where to pick up a package for Kasha and where to drop off his son to him. After this, he swore I was of my leash. I had proven to Raul that I wasn't a snitch and that J would never resurface. He had booked a flight for two out of the country, one way, and had two million waiting for me once the exchange was made. All I had to do was fulfill my part. And with Dottie gone, I needed someone to spend my eternity with. Luckily for me, I knew just the chick. I had flown out my Miami jump for the week, thinking we would have this time to spend together. But no, Kasha had me wrapped up in her sick games. I was done with that entire family, for real.

I pulled up to Hilton and headed to the suite I had booked in my name. I walked in and found different shopping bags all over the place. Clearly, she had been having fun with my credit card. I closed the door and realized I heard the shower running. My dick instantly stood at attention at the thought of

Ayana naked with water dripping down her curves. I took off my clothes with my fully erect snake out and ready. I walked towards the shower and quietly crept inside behind her. I took in her naked frame for a few seconds before making my presence known. She jumped at the feeling of me against her cheeks. She jumped and turned to my grinning face.

"Nigga, the fuck you thought?" she spat at me as she grabbed for her towel and headed out of the shower. The water started to hit me in the face as I called out to her in confusion, but she just kept walking.

Fuck it! I'm already in here, might as well clean my   balls. Once I was clean, I got out and wrapped a towel around my body. I found Ayana fully dressed in the room and packing her bags. I could tell she had an attitude.

"What's your problem?" I asked her as if I didn't know.

"O'har, what the fuck did you fly me down here for? I could have went shopping by myself in Miami. What did you bring me out here for?" she barked at me.

I turned my head sideways to study this girl like she was stupid. You see, I had been dealing with Ayana for a few months now. I had started fucking her a few months back. I had actually grown feelings for her. She was sexy and had a lot of attitude. Plus, she loved spending money just as much as I loved making it. I wanted to get out of the game, and she would make the perfect trophy wife. But she acted like she hadn't had fun just blowing my money and taking my private jet out here. *Who was she trying to fool?*

"Look, baby, I had a lot of last-minute business to handle. But I'm almost done with it. I have a huge surprise for you. I just got to wrap some shit up."

I tried to give her the run around. I didn't involve Ayana in my business because I didn't want her becoming a casualty of war. Nobody knew about her, and I was trying to keep it that way.

She sucked her teeth and tossed her hands up at me. "Your actin' just like the last nigga I was mixed up with. You never want to be seen in public with me. You just wanna give me the money and fuck me. You probably got a wife just like I found out that nigga do!" Ayana hollered while jabbing her finger in my face.

I rolled my eyes and picked up a cigar to spark. I was over her talking about this Miami nigga she was hooked on. I thought for sure after she caught him in the club with another girl, that I wouldn't have to hear about this nigga, again. As soon as I was done with Raul, I would make a pit stop and find this nigga, Yayo, and kill him so she would finally shut up about it. "Look, Ayana, I already told you I'ma handle that nigga for you. I just need to finish this business. Then I'll body the nigga, myself. Now, if you're ready to go home, I have Ricardo fire up the plane for you and we can go. Just say the word," I said. I was done arguing with her.

A smile spread across her face and she loosened up.

"So, you really gone kill him for me?" she asked.

"Yes, baby. You just gotta get him to ya crib and I'll end his shit. Nobody disrespects you," I said. She kissed me and we went over the plan. After an hour of fucking, we were carrying her many bags down to the car and headed to the airport; looking like a ghetto married couple and shit. We were on the flyway to board out flight back to Miami when my phone began to go off. It was Kasha. I rolled my eyes as I told the driver to pull over. I couldn't risk Ayana hearing any of this shit. Even though she had fallen asleep, one never really knows with her.

"What the fuck do you want, Kasha?" I whispered into the phone as I stood outside of the whip. I was over this whole damn situation. She had gone too far with kidnapping Raul's son, and I wanted no parts of the shit.

"Hey, O'har," she sounded so sweet over the phone.

"I just wanted to say that I thank you for helping me find out what happened to my aunty. She was lucky to have you. Listen, I'm sending Raul's son home. Come get him from Auntie's house. He'll be waiting outside. Raul gave me a location to bring him. You should hurry, though. If the police drive by and see a child outside like this at night, they might take him and Raul might not be happy about that."

Click!

I couldn't believe this shit! I chocked the phone before taking some deep breaths. I had no choice but to make a detour and get this kid. Kasha texted me the address and I had the driver head that way. I just hoped like hell that Ayana would stay asleep the entire time while this was going down, Though I doubted it. I didn't want her asking too many questions. I was completely over this life and this fucking game.

I pulled up and scooped up Junior. He was a happy kid to be so mixed up in his father's bullshit. He had a backpack like the day he had been picked up. He didn't talk much, he just kept repeating something in his broken English

"Give papa bag, bye. Give Pap bag, bye."

I didn't bother talking to him. I just wanted to drop him off and be over all of this.

Once we arrived at the location, my anxiety skyrocketed. Raul was standing outside of this massive compound with a bunch of shooters standing behind him. My heart dropped into my nuts and I started to sweat. I looked over junior to make sure he wasn't injured. I knew if even a paper cut was on this boy, that was going to be somebody's ass. I got out first and every gun was pointed at me I raised my hands high in the air and Junior stepped out beside me.

"Papa!" he yelled out of joy.

I saw Raul smile and that shit took me out. I never seen this ruthless man show any type of emotions. He got down on his knees and embraced his son. It felt like an eternity before he let him go and signaled one of his men to approach me. This big linebacker looking' ass man approached me with a satin box with a crown on it and handed it to me.

"Boss says don't ever show your face in the states, again," the man said coldly as he handed me an envelope.

I could still hear Junior repeating the same thing, happily while his father picked him and his backpack up. I quickly got back in the car an exhaled.

I sat the box in the front seat with the driver before going through the envelope to see what was in it. A smile spread across my face when I saw the two passports with both Ayana's and mines faces on them. There was also the information for two offshore accounts with my money in it. I fell back in my seat and let out a sigh of relief. The shit was finally   over! My phone began to ring, and it was Kasha. I was happy that this would be the last time I would be hearing from this psychopath and her family.

"I did it, alright. Now stop calling me. We are done," I proudly whispered into the phone.

"Did Raul like his package?" Kasha spoke into the phone. I looked at the phone in confusion. "What? His son? No shit. I just dropped him..."

Boom!

The entire car shook. I looked out the window and saw that the house had exploded.

"Oh shit! Drive, nigga. Drive!" I demanded my driver.

Without missing a beat, my driver sped off. I watched the property become engulfed in flames behind us. My heart was bouncing out of my chest as I turned back in my seat and brought the phone to my head.

"What... what the fuck have you done?" I asked.

Kasha gave me a wicked laugh. "You're almost out of the game, O'har. But not completely. Bring my auntie's head back to Miami, and we'll be done, my nigga."

Click!

I looked at my phone and then at the ceiling. What the fuck was she talking about? I didn't know where that woman's head was.... My heart stopped a second as my eyes landed on the box Raul had given me.

She wouldn't!

I looked at Ayana to make sure she was still sound asleep before having my driver pull over, again. I got out of the car and pulled the box out from the front seat. I quickly opened it and realized that I did know where her head was. I quickly tucked the box back in the car and ordered my driver to head towards the airport. I was going to deliver this head and be down with Kasha. This bitch was clearly more than I wanted to deal with. Ayana was just going to have to accept the new plan. We were not staying in Miami for long. I was making this drop, and then we were   leaving.

****

Ayana wasn't happy about me leaving her at her house while I went out and tied up some loose ends. She was asking me a thousand and one fucking questions and I didn't feel like answering any of them for her. I was riding around the 305 with a fucking head in my trunk. I just needed this shit to be over. I punched in the location Kasha told me to bring her the package to. I really wanted this girl to disappear. However, I had more respect for Dottie than to kill her niece. Ha! The irony in that shit was real. A hypocritical statement I was taking to my grave.

Kasha Diaz

I drove for an hour before I reached the rendezvous spot. It turned out to be an underground parking garage that was dimly lit. I pulled into it with caution and reached for my burned under the seat. Kasha had proven she was not to be fucked with. She had done what many had been too afraid to even dream about. She took out the King of the cartel. She had crossed old lines and murdered a child to do it. To do that, you had to be dark. So, I knew if it came down to it, ironic respect or not, I would have to light her up. I rode down to find Kasha standing in an all-black long dress that was skintight on her body. She didn't have a bag on her at all. Her dress was so tight that I was for sure that there was no way she had that thang on her. So, I tucked mine by my side before parking and killed the engine. I tried to study her, but I got nothing.

I pulled the box from my passenger seat and stepped out with it extended from my body. Kasha made eye contact with it, and I almost saw a crack in her poker face. I set the box down at her feet and watched her cock her neck around before exhaling.

"Look, Kasha. I'm really sorry for your loss. I loved Dottie, but I knew what time it was when it came to stepping to Raul. She went out like a soldier, and I know you made her proud. But I'm out of the game for good," I said.

She nodded. "Yeah, I know. I just had to get back at Raul for ordering this hit on my ken folks," she said in a cold tone.

"I understand," I said as I looked down one last time at the box. I kept thinking how that could have been me or anyone. But it wasn't. "That's the thing about that nigga Raul, though," Kasha said. I wasn't interested in talking to her anymore, though, so I said nothing.

"Raul makes the calls, but…"

Click Clack!

I looked up to see twenty guns coming out of the darkness and pointed at me. I completely froze up as the sound of heels behind me crept closer and closer.

"But somebody else did the work. Somebody got close enough to my auntie Dottie to stab her in the back and cut her fucking head off."

WHOP!

Chapter 15

Kasha

I was taught that the key to the game was to stay one step ahead of everybody and account for every move. I told my niggas that some niggas played checkers and some played chess. We were them niggas that played chess. I knew someone close to Aunty had done her in. But I knew O'har was guilty from the moment he opened his mouth. My big brother taught me that some people listen to hear rather than listen to comprehend. I learned early that niggas will snitch on themselves without you having to apply much pressure.

O'har was saying *was* when he talked about my Aunty like he knew she was dead before I even said anything. Before we walked into that room where we found her beheaded, he was getting himself ready for the smell of a decaying body like he knew it was there. *To add to that*, Raul didn't smoke his ass even though he said he dropped Raul as his connect. That nigga did it and it was time to pay for it. He was loyal to the wrong side, period!

We pulled back up to the house and Yayo met me at the door. A part of me wanted to fall into his arms, but now still wasn't the time. He had his men take Auntie's remains to the funeral home he bought me in her honor to have her head cremated. I made the order to let Product wake up. Tomorrow was the day I would have to give him the bad news. I still wasn't sure how I was going to do that shit.

We stayed up all night waiting on Auntie's remains to come back to me. When they did, they were in a gold and diamond studded urn with her name embroidered on it. I held them close to me as tears began to slide down my face. I wished like hell I didn't have to do this. But once I got the word the next day that he was awake, there was no more time to wish for. I kissed the urn one last time. Raul was dead, but now I had to do the hardest thing I had to do since this war started. Yayo tried to hand me the blunt, but I turned it down. I had some raw emotions in me, and if they were going to come out, now was the time.

We walked up to the room where Product was recovering. He was now awake and able to talk and understand everything. When he saw me, he smiled and walked from the bed to meet me.

"Hey, fav! I was starting to think you abandon me," he joked.

I laughed and hugged him back. "Never that," I said in a low tone. It was all over my face that something was wrong.

"What's good, Kasha? You mad about the shipment. We gone get those niggas. If I know my momma, she probably handling that shit right now," he boasted with pride. It felt like I had just been punched in my chest.

I looked at Yayo and Ram, and they looked sad and ready for what was about to happen. I couldn't find the words, so I just handed him the urn. He looked at it confused and wouldn't take it.

"Kash, who… who is this?" he asked me.

I began to choke on the knot in my throat. "Cousin... it's your mom.... Ra… Raul had her killed. I got her cremated for you," I stuttered. The tears began to fall down my face and wouldn't stop.

Product slowly took the box and looked at it in disbelief. "Nah! Fuck that shit! This ain't my mom's, my nigga!" he hollered and almost smashed the urn. I quickly stopped him and told him it wasn't a lie.

"I'm so sorry..." I cried out.

Product's chest pumped in and out as he tried so hard not to cry.

"I'ma kill that muthafucka!" he screamed.

"You can't, cousin. I killed Raul," I told him.

He looked at me with anger in his eyes. "You what? You what? No! That was my kill, Kasha. That niggas blood belonged to me!" he growled as he clutched his chest.

I snapped my finger and a nurse emerged with a needle in her hand. Product looked at the needle then back at me.

"What the fuck is this shit?" he cried out to me.

"It's concentrated steroids and adrenaline. You are still weak, my nigga. This will give you strength like the Hulk," I explained.

Product began to laugh and sat the urn down on the bed he had been laid up in for days.

"What do I need that for?" he asked me with tears rolling down his cheeks.

I smiled with my face covered in tears. "Cousin, I killed Raul. But not the person that pulled the trigger. I left that for you." I said.

I turned and opened the door. Three of our men drug O'har in, cuffed, gagged, and strung him up on metal hook that was hanging from the ceiling. Product's eyes got huge as he watched this go down.

"This is the muthafucka that Aunty trusted with her heart. He cut her fucking head off to make a deal with Raul to get out of the game. Raul sent a picture of Auntie's head out to all of our allies and they all left us. He left the rest of Auntie's body to rot in her home. Then he helped Raul rob us and leave you for dead!"

Ram and Yayo walked out of the room as Product took in everything, I had said to him.

"Give me that fucking shot," he said in a cold and low tone.

O'har's eyes bugged out of its sockets as the medicine went straight into Product's veins.

"One more thing, my nigga," Ram said as he entered the room. He put a rolled-up leather blanket in front of Product and unrolled it to show an arsenal of sharp and deadly weapons inside of it. A wicked smile spread across.my cousins face before I exited the room. Whatever was about to happen to that nigga was too good for him.

*****

Yayo

In Love with the Queen of SC

Nothing was the same after Kasha got her revenge. Word got out about what she had done, and everyone began to fall in line. Soon, Kasha wasn't just running Miami, but just about everywhere. She had her hands in more than just the drug game. She had dealings with the F.B.I., Politicians, and even foreign drug rings. Her ass even had a sit down with the Russians. She was doing more than she had ever envisioned. Her aunty would be extremely proud of her. She was on some real Queen Pin shit. The Black Griselda Blanca had arrived.

Unfortunately, the same could not be said for us. We had gotten matching whips and loyalty tattoos. We were officially an item, but we were constantly getting into it. She was constantly pushing me away and I couldn't figure out why. But whenever she would start, I would just leave. I didn't want to argue with her. I knew she was grieving. But a nigga could only take so much more shit. I was ready for us to be official. I wanted to marry her ass. I had a ring for her too. I wanted to give her my mom's ring. But then that shit dawned on me that Ayana had taken that shit the last time I saw her.

It was late at night and Kasha was in a good mood. We had gone out the entire day without any arguing. I loved seeing that girl smile. I had the entire engagement set up with a special surprise for her. But now, I needed that damn ring. I didn't want to, but I called Ayana to let her know I was on my way to her house. I didn't feel like arguing with her or her fucking up my good vibe. I knew that she wouldn't give me the ring if she knew it was for somebody else, so I left that part out of the phone call. I hurried up and started getting dressed.

As I headed out of the stairs, I heard Kasha yell from behind me.

"So, you really can't let that bitch go?".

I turned to see her standing at the top of the stairs. She looked crazy in the face and I knew that it was about to be some shit.

"Kasha, whatever you're mad about, we can talk about it later. I'll be back," I said as I headed down the stairs. I was shocked that she was following right behind me.

"No, Yayo. We gone talk about this shit right now. I been ignoring the shit but I'm fucking tired. I saw you with another bitch at the club the night that Product was robbed. I know that's who you were just on the phone with and I know that's where you are finna go. Is that where you been creeping off to every fucking night?" she hollered. I could hear the braking in her voice.

I didn't even know what to say. I had forgotten about the whole club shit. Anyways there wasn't nothing to tell. So, why was she even on this? I never would have pegged Kasha to be the jealous type. Especially not over no random ass bitch that could not hold a light to her. But I knew my baby girl and I knew my words wouldn't really mean shit to her without some actions.

"Kash, look. I'm not going to argue with you. I'm not seeing no other bitch. I know you are still grieving over your aunty and I..."

Smack!

I held my face and the sting almost had me seeing red. I was raised to never put my hands on a woman, but it was free reign on any bitch that hit me like she was a man. Still, I just couldn't bring myself to do Kasha in that type of way. I huffed hard and caught my composure as she began to scream at me.

"Don't bring her up. I'm not fucking crazy. You tryna do me like all these other niggas. What? Are you gonna kill me like O'har did my Aunty, too?" she hollered.

I got to admit that shit hurt me to my core. I couldn't believe that she would think I would do something like that. That type of action wasn't even close to the type of nigga I was. I knew she was hurting, but damn! I just couldn't face her at the moment, so I left. She kept coming behind me; screaming and making accusations. I got into my car and began to drive off. I could hear her saying stuff about being a made bitch, but I didn't stop. I had shit to handle. I wasn't going to end the night like this.

In Love with the Queen of SC

******

Ayana.

I should have figured this nigga would go ghost on me. It had been months since I last heard from O'har and I had grown impatient. The flight that we had booked for us to leave the country was for tomorrow and a bitch was done waiting. I had the pin to the offshore accounts he had set up for us. I wasn't the type of bitch to ask too many questions. I didn't love O'har, to be completely honest. But I loved his bread and how naive the nigga was. He was my meal ticket up out of Hialeah, and I was riding with that. I didn't know what this nigga was caught up in and I didn't want to know. He fucked up by leaving me all of the paperwork for us to leave. I was never crazy about leaving the country with his ass, but now I could leave this bitch, alone and with millions waiting on me. *Single in a different country?* Not bad for an around the way girl.

I sat with my shit all packed in the backseat of my Mazda 6. I had Nipsy's *Double Up* playing as I finished my last American blunt. I was waiting on Yayo. I knew eventually he would try to weasel his way back to me, but not this time. Yayo was a dope dude and a good ticket for me, but I was not about to keep fucking around with these drugs dealing ass niggas. I lost my daddy to the game and my mom became an addict. I did not aspire to be like her in no way and that meant cutting off these sketchy ass dudes like O'har and Yayo.

Word around town was that the head of the Cartel had blown up by some wanna be Griselda and I had no time for that shit. The way I see it, God was giving my way out and I would be a super dumb broad to ignore it. But that meant saying goodbye to Yayo, for good. Which meant giving him back the ring he had from his mom. He never officially gave me the ring, but I felt like it belonged to me at some point. He didn't know that I was about to give it back and I just hoped he took the shit, peacefully. I was ready for the start of my new life on new soul. I wanted to reinvent myself as a new woman and away from my past. I was done fucking niggas who didn't love me to get by. I was done being the typical project chick. God was giving me a second chance. And I was ready for that shit.

Chapter 16

I couldn't believe I had put my hands on Yayo. I knew there was no coming back from that. I was surprised I was still breathing. He must have really loved me because had I been another female, I would be a cold shell in a black bag, period! But at this point, I realized that I needed to get away. My emotions were out of fucking wack and I couldn't deal with this, right now.

I hurried upstairs and packed me up a couple of things. I booked me a room at the Eden Roc and drove myself. I decided I was going to stay there for a few nights and let things die down. I left Yayo a note on the door bedside table.

Once I hopped into my car and had my bags in the trunk, I called Ram and Product and let them know that I was going off of the grid for a few and for them to hold shit down. I knew it wasn't the responsible thing for me to step out of the way while we were on the rise, but it was needed. I was becoming unhinged and that shit was just not me.

Maybe there was some truth to what Yayo was saying, or maybe there wasn't. All I knew was that I couldn't figure things out here. I pulled my battery out of my cell phone and drove with 6Lack *Cutting Ties* blasting through the speakers.

I'll tell you what you wanna know
When it comes to cutting ties
girl I'm like a pro!

For the next two days, I didn't leave my hotel room. I didn't eat, I didn't shower I didn't do anything but cry and slept. That void finally hit me. I was going through the stages of grief. I was reflecting on everything that had happened and it was kicking my ass. I kept seeing the face of Raul Jr in my dreams and it shook me to my core. The first night, I had a dream that I was as in hell with the heads of my enemies surrounding me. I never was too religious, but that shit shook me to my core!

By the third day, I was tired of feeling this way. I started doing research on sage. My Aunty used to burn sage back in the day, and I used to think she was off of her rocker, but maybe there was something to this *energy* shit. So, On the third day, I got on Google and found a pop-up shop down in Pembroke Pines. I got dressed in a hot pink joggers' suit from *Fashion Nova*, swiped my *Prada* shades from off the dresser and slicked my hair into a neat bun before heading out.

I ended up at a shop called Sole Luna ran by an elder woman named Giya. She was very sweet and put me up on game. I ended up leaving with Three bundles of sage, a feather and some lavender. I bought some candles and incents too. When I got back to the room, I ordered me some food and drank some wine. That night, I meditated and had some of the best sleep I ever had. For the rest of the week, I was on and off of the beach; soaking in the sun and enjoying the waves. I was starting to miss Yayo and realized my feelings for him were deeper than I wanted to ever admit. It was time for me to go home to my man.

*****

Yayo

By now you know the type of bitch that I am. I'm not the type to admit when I'm wrong or hurting or even lonely. I knew that getting physical with you was very wrong. You may be right. I may be holding onto the pain of losing my Aunty. I don't know what is going on with me, but I plan to find out. When I saw you with that girl, I lost it. I immediately felt like you were trying to play me. You're the first nigga to see me be vulnerable and I don't want to be betrayed like Aunty was... I'm going to go and

get my head clear for a few days and I'll be back
next weekend. I'm not sure what or where we will be
by then, but I do want to say that I do not want to
lose you...
-Kasha...

My girl had been gone for a week, but I was ready for her come back. I had thought long and hard about everything that Kasha and I had been through since we first met. From the jump, she had a wall up and remained a gangsta. It took a lot to get to see the real her, and a nigga really fell in love with all of her. I didn't know what to make out of her slapping me. I had never had a woman test me in that way. But I understood. Kasha had spent her whole life being strong that she didn't know how to handle all of this loss and stress she had endured. I wanted to be there for her and it was high time that shawty understood that.

It was about five in the evening when Kasha pulled up. I was nervous as fuck, but I was ready for baby girl to know how I felt. She walked slowly into the house and saw me standing at the top of the stairs. Our eyes met and I could see the vulnerability in her. I loved it.

She slowly began to speak. I could tell that she was nervous. "Yayo, look, I'm really-"

Before she could finish, a woman in a bartender's outfit emerged from the kitchen with a smile on her face. Just as I suspected, Kasha twisted her face up at the woman and then back at me. It took everything in me not burst out laughing. I could imagine Kasha going crazy on that ass, real quick. I was hoping everything pan out the way it was supposed   to.

*****

Kasha

I didn't know what to expect when I finally drove home. I walked into the door and saw Yayo standing there, so you know I sure as shit didn't expect for some random thot to be walking up to me in my own home. She approached me with a goofy looking smile. This bitch just didn't know that I was about to be laying her out and smacking that smile straight off of her face.

"He said have a good time," she said as she handed me a bottle of Rose.

The woman walked off as I looked from the bottle to Yayo. I immediately began to smile, and he smiled back.

"Send this back!" I said with a smile. He began to laugh as I slowly walked up the steps towards him. I took his sexy stature in with every step I took. Yayo was beyond fine

Everything about him was a straight panty droppa.

"Damn, ma. So, you just gone send my bottle back?" he said as he bit his bottom lip and pulled me closer to him.

"You know I don't drink that cheap shit," I said as I wrapped my arms around his neck. He kissed me on the lips and I felt that same shock I got when we first kissed.

"Is that right?" he asked me as he pulled me by the booty close to his frame.

"Mhmm," I moaned into his chest.

"Well, if you won't accept my bottle, will you accept my ring?" he asked me.

I backed up and looked him up and down in confusion. "What? What did you just say?" I whispered.

"You heard me, Queen. I love you, Kasha. You are my equal. You not gone have my back, you gone be right by my side. I don't ever wanna be without you. Baby, I love you, G," he hit me with the goofiest smile I've ever seen. He stood back and took me in. "But I can't give you this ring, without asking a special person for his blessing," he continued to smile.

I was completely confused as the master bedroom down flung open. My jaw damn near fell off and my knees almost gave out from under me. I couldn't believe who I was seeing. This shit had to be a prank.

"Big Brother?" I cried out.

He sped walked up to me with that same beautiful smile and hugged me tight. I couldn't believe my brother; Duval was standing in front of me.

"How?" I cried out loud as hell as my tears stained my brother's shirt.

"Yo boy Yayo had some words with the DA. Turns out, they had false evidence that led to my conviction. All of the information the FBI had on Raul had subsequently disappeared. When it came out that the FBI gave their files to Raul, they tried to break into his compound. Only to find out it had burned in a house fire, along with Raul and his men. The judge dismissed the charges and Product came to get me," My big brother explained.

"Oh My God!" I hollered out in happiness. "The sage works!"

They both looked at each other confused before laughing.

"Aye bro, I believe you had something you wanted to talk to me about?" My brother addressed Yayo. I looked up from him to my man.

"Yeah, bruh. I wanted to let you know that your baby sister is the most beautiful and amazing woman on this planet. And, I really want to spoil her for the rest of her life," Yayo stated.

My brother puffed air before laughing. "You know she don't need you to do none of that. She's self-made!" My brother boasted.

Yayo laughed and agreed. "I know. But I want to. I want this self-made Queen to be with a self-made King. I want to ask you for your blessing as the head man in her life, and to give us your blessing so I can ask her will she marry me?"

Yayo was now down on one knee with a ring box in his hands. I began to cry all over again. truth be told, I didn't even wait for my brother to give an answer. I jumped into Yayo's arms and screamed that I would. They both began to laugh as my brother brought up that I was so self-made that I didn't even need his approval. And he was right, because I truly was a made bitch!

And a Made Bitch makes her own moves!

The End!

Kasha Diaz

Coming soon!

**I Messed Up My Life
How Do I Fix It?**

Kasha has had her fair share of hiccups in her thirty plus years of living. In this powerful, yet veracious self care narrative, she unpacks her trials and tribulations.

She takes the reader through verifiable accounts of her life. With the ups comes the downs. So, she doesn't restrain from stating her shortcomings. She expresses what she has learned while she scuffled with misplaced anger, self doubt, heart break, and misfortune.

Although her journey isn't nearly complete, she felt compelled to inspire young America and give them insight on how she now manages depression, anxiety, a restless mind, and mishaps.

She gives her personal advice on "how to keep it moving." Which seems to be hard when the cards are against you.

I Messed Up My Life
How Do I Fix It?

A SELF-HELP AFFIRMATION BY
Kasha Diaz

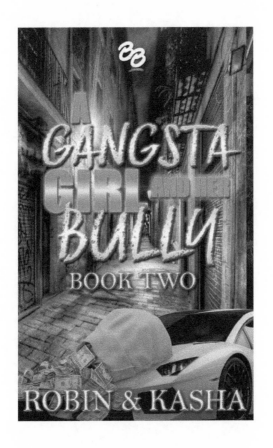

Contact the Author

Facebook Author Kasha Diaz

IG: kasha_Diaz